Clint rose as another ninja
entered . . . .

The killer in black hissed like a snake as he slashed a sword at the Gunsmith's head. Clint didn't have time to work the lever action of his carbine. He raised the Springfield and held it up like a bar to block the attacking blade.

Clint turned sharply and delivered a butt-stroke across the ninja's arms. The blow struck the sword from his opponent's grasp, but the ninja swiftly snap-kicked Clint in the gut.

The ninja grabbed the gun and pulled it across the Gunsmith's throat. The bastard was trying to throttle Clint with his own gun . . . .

Don't miss any of the lusty, hard-riding action in the
Charter Western series, THE GUNSMITH

And coming next month:

THE GUNSMITH #44: THE SCARLET GUN

THE GUNSMITH

43

THE GOLDEN HORSEMAN

J.R. ROBERTS

CHARTER BOOKS, NEW YORK

THE GUNSMITH #43: THE GOLDEN HORSEMAN

A Charter Book/published by arrangement with
the author

PRINTING HISTORY
Charter edition/August 1985

ISBN: 0-441-30947-X

Charter Books are published by The Berkley Publishing Group,
200 Madison Avenue, New York, New York 10016.
PRINTED IN THE UNITED STATES OF AMERICA

To Richard Curtis

ONE

Clint Adams tightened the bolts to the stock of the Winchester. He had replaced a broken spring mechanism to the hammer. Clint cocked the hammer and kept his left thumb on it as he squeezed the trigger. The hammer moved forward smoothly. Clint eased it into place. Of course, the rifle was not loaded. One always double-checks a weapon to be certain it's not loaded before attempting to repair it. However, Clint believed one can never be too careful when handling a gun, and he always obeyed the basic rule of firearm safety. Always treat a weapon as if it's loaded. That's the best way to avoid accidents.

Clint Adams was a gunsmith by chosen profession. He had been labeled ''the Gunsmith'' years ago when he was still a deputy sheriff. A newspaper man had decided to write a story about the young lawman who had already acquired an unwanted reputation as a fast gun. Indeed, Clint Adams was incredibly fast and accurate with a gun, perhaps the best pistolman who ever lived. However, the journalist needed something to make his story more color-ful. Some personal character trait about Deputy Adams which would make him unusual among the other ''living legends of the West.''

The news hound discovered that Clint was not only an

1

expert gunman, but also an amateur gunsmith. The deputy had an uncanny talent with firearms, and he was adept at repairing and modifying guns as a hobby. In fact, Clint had converted a single action .45 caliber Colt revolver to fire double-action. Deputy Adams had first learned about this innovation from reading about British-made double-action or self-cocking revolvers. After two years of trial and error, he succeeded in modifying the Colt which became his regular sidearm and constant companion.

The journalist immediately jumped on Clint's hobby as the unique element needed for his story, and he labeled Deputy Adams "the Gunsmith." The monicker would eventually make Clint Adams famous. It also ruined his career as a lawman.

Clint discovered his new reputation was quite a burden to bear. Young gunhawks came after him, eager for a chance at fame as the "man who killed the Gunsmith." Clint avoided these confrontations whenever possible, but sometimes the youthful gunslingers forced his hand. So more young gunhawks wound up in Boot Hill, and the legend of the Gunsmith continued to grow.

The public was also a problem. Half the population seemed to regard Clint Adams as a gun-crazy lawman with a license to kill. Everybody else seemed to expect Clint to handle every problem with his six-gun and they were always disappointed when he didn't. Clint decided he could no longer do his job, and he turned in his badge after eighteen years as a deputy.

Clint then loaded up a wagon and began to drift across the country. His only companion and partner was a magnificent black Arabian gelding named Duke. Eight hundred pounds of muscle, intelligence, courage, and loyalty, Duke was the strongest, fastest, and smartest horse the Gunsmith had ever owned. Clint valued the gelding more

than his modified Colt revolver, more than anything—
except his own life.

The ultimate irony was the fact that Clint Adams was
qualified for only two types of work, so when he turned in
his badge, he became a traveling gunsmith. He roamed
from town to town and state to state, repairing and modifying weapons for a living. Clint's life-style was free and
independent. It allowed him to see a lot of the United
States without being accountable to anyone except himself.

A traveling gunsmith might seem to be a fairly peaceful
and quiet life, but Clint always seemed to find more than
his share of adventure wherever he went. Sometimes this
was due to coincidence and happenstance, yet the
Gunsmith often got involved in such situations due to his
own actions. Clint was very curious by nature and he
really enjoyed a bit of adventure from time to time. He
also still had a strong sense of justice, and when he came
upon corruption or injustice, Clint still felt obliged to do
something about it.

"Well, your owner ought to be happy with you now,"
Clint told the Winchester as he propped it against the wall
beside his desk in the hotel room. "And that wraps up
business for another day."

The Gunsmith had repaired three rifles, one shotgun,
and four pistols. Not a bad amount of business considering
how small the town of Lawton, California was. Clint was
pleased with his visit to Lawton. He had not only made a
decent profit, but he'd also met a charming young lady at
the general store who had agreed to have dinner with him
that night.

Clint decided to head over to the barber shop for a shave
and a haircut before it was time to meet Alice Walters at
the store. She'd told him she closed the shop at five and

wanted another hour to get ready, so Clint had plenty of time. He might even stop by the local saloon for a cold brew first. The summer heat was enough to make a lizard thirsty.

The Gunsmith left his room and descended the staircase to the lobby below. The desk clerk gazed up at him fearfully. Clint Adams was a handsome man. He was tall and lean with brown eyes and dark hair. A jagged scar marred his left cheek. It was the only evidence that Clint was experienced with violence—unless one noticed that he wore his Colt pistol low on his hip, like a professional gunfighter.

Of course, the desk clerk knew who Clint Adams was. He had heard of the Gunsmith's reputation, and he wasn't certain if Clint was a threat or not. The Gunsmith hadn't done anything to make the desk clerk suspicious, but he didn't have to. The fellow knew that Clint had become a legend because of his skill with a gun. That was enough to make the clerk nervous.

"Howdy, Mr. Adams," the man said with an unsteady voice. "Anything wrong with the room? I mean, if there is, I can give you another one."

"The room's fine," Clint assured him. "I'm just going out for a while, friend. Worked all day and now I can relax a little. Know what I mean?"

"Well, I'm not sure how you like to relax, Mr. Adams," the clerk replied. He immediately regretted his choice of words. "But I'm sure you have a good time and it ain't none of my business what you do."

"Don't worry," the Gunsmith assured him, "I promise not to burn down the town."

Clint stepped out of the hotel onto the plankwalk. He glanced about at the simple, practical wooden structures which comprised the town of Lawton. It looked like a hundred other small towns he'd seen in a dozen states in the past. The one unusual feature was a railroad running along the south end of town.

A train was parked on the tracks. The locomotive didn't appear to be very large. Only six or seven cars were linked behind a diamond-stack engine. The train was probably privately owned. It certainly couldn't carry much cargo or livestock.

A curious oddity, the train didn't concern the Gunsmith. He headed for the local saloon and pushed through the batwings. The tavern was also rather typical for a small town in the West. The bar was a simple wooden counter with shelves of whiskey and kegs of beer behind it. The floor was laced with sawdust, and the tables and chairs were simple and practical. A weary, heavy-set bartender stood behind the counter. Five cowboys sat at one table. They laughed and joked as they gulped down shots of red-eye.

Clint noticed that two of the cowhands were arm wrestling while the other three watched, no doubt betting on who would win. To make the match more interesting, candles had been set at both sides of the struggling arms. As one contestant gained the advantage, he pulled the back of his opponent's hand toward the flame of one of the candles. The Gunsmith figured the cow-pokes could entertain themselves anyway they wanted so long as they didn't harm anyone else. They were all full-grown, and if they thought it was funny to burn each other's hands, then let them play their dumbass games and count their blisters later.

"How'd business go, Clint?" the bartender inquired.

"Not bad," the Gunsmith replied as he approached the bar. "Say, isn't that side-by-side Greener shotgun yours?"

"That's a fact," the bartender confirmed. "Did you happen to get around to fixin' it, Clint?"

"Yeah," Clint nodded. "I should have brought it to you, but I forgot. I'm afraid I don't remember your name either, friend."

"That's all right," the barman said with a shrug. "Reckon you talked to a lot of fellers today. Name's Jack Pearson."

"Well, Jack," Clint began. "I'll get your Greener to you before sunset, if that's soon enough."

"Wouldn't mind havin' it sooner," Jack replied; he tilted his head toward the cowboys at the table. "Them fellers from the Double J Ranch can get a might rowdy."

"If it'll make you feel better," the Gunsmith said. "I can go get the shotgun for you right now."

"Much obliged, Clint," the bartender said. "But I reckon I can wait long enough for you to have a beer. Mighty hot day for you to be crossin' the street without some cold brew in your belly."

"You talked me into it," the Gunsmith grinned.

One of the cowboys suddenly screamed. Clint glanced over his shoulder. The unfortunate cowhand was holding his burned right hand, teeth clenched in pain. The others laughed and congratulated the winner of the arm-wrestling contest.

"This place is sure a lot of fun," the Gunsmith muttered as Jack placed a mug of beer on the bar.

"What the hell is that?" a cowboy exclaimed, staring at the batwings.

Clint turned to see what the man referred to. He wasn't sure what he was looking at either. A man had entered the saloon. He was dressed in a silk robe and some sort of baggy trousers with wooden sandals on his feet. His sideburns were long, but the top of his head was shaved except for a tuft of black hair bound by a gold band. A crimson sash was wrapped around his narrow waist.

Two swords were thrust in the man's sash, one about four feet long and the other roughly half that length. The swords were sheathed in polished wooden scabbards. The hafts of the weapons were wrapped in sharkskin and braided black silk. The handguards were wide and circular, adorned with ornate designs.

The stranger's face was lean with high cheekbones and dark, almond-shaped eyes. Clint was certain the man was Oriental, but he didn't resemble anyone he had encountered in San Francisco's Chinatown.*

"Hey, are you with the carnival, fella?" one of the cowboys laughed. "Sure look like somethin' from a freak show."

"Looks like a she-boy to me," a big bruiser declared. "Dressed up in skirts and all." He was the winner of the arm-wrestling contest. Obviously, he was used to saying what he pleased to anyone he didn't figure would shoot him.

"How about it, fella?" a lanky cowhand with buckteeth began. He had a remarkable resemblance to a jackass even before he spoke. "You like to bed down with boys, feller?"

"No, thank you," the stranger said slowly, his accent adding a sharpness to every vowel he uttered. "But please do whatever you wish to one another."

"What's he mean by that?" the jackass wondered.

The stranger walked to the bar. He noticed a wiry grin on the Gunsmith's face. He nodded curtly at Clint, who returned the gesture. Jack the bartender glanced from the newcomer to the five cowboys, clearly more concerned about the latter.

---

*Gunsmith #27: Chinatown Hell

"You are the innkeeper, yes?" the stranger inquired.

"Innkeeper?" Jack frowned. "This here is a saloon, feller. If'n you want a drink, I can oblige you. If you want a room, go see the hotel folks."

"A drink will be fine, please," the man assured him.

"Beer or whiskey?" Jack asked.

"Beer," the stranger replied as if uncertain what he had just ordered. "Beer, please. Yes?"

"Where'd you learn to speak American, boy?" the big cowboy said as he rose from his chair. "Didn't teach you too good, China boy."

The stranger stiffened. He turned slowly to face the cowhands, his eyes hard as black stone. The muscles of his face tensed with anger.

"I am not Chinese," he announced. "I am Kaiju Inoshiro of the samurai *rentai* of Lord Nagata. *Wakarimasu desu*? Do you understand?"

"All I understand is you're one of them yellow boys," the bully snorted. "And a goddamn slant-eyes ain't got no right bein' in a white man's saloon."

"This fella isn't hurting anyone, mister," the Gunsmith declared. "Why don't you just sit down and leave him be?"

"You mind your own business, asshole," the brute growled. "Unless you want another scar on the other side of your face."

"Shit, Errol," Jack said quickly. "Don't you know who you're talkin' to? This here is Clint Adams."

"The Gunsmith?" Errol stared at Clint as if he'd just encountered a cougar in his bedroll.

"Some folks call me that," Clint confirmed calmly, dropping his right to the Colt on his hip.

"Er . . . no offense meant," Errol said awkwardly.

"But I don't know why you want'a stick up for this chink."

"I am Japanese," Kaiju stated angrily. "I am samurai."

"You're a fish-face yellow boy," the big cowboy snapped. "Now, get your ass outta this saloon before I blow your friggin' head off!"

Errol's hand reached for his six-gun. The Gunsmith's Colt appeared in his hand so fast nobody even saw the blur of his arm when he drew the revolver. Errol froze and slowly raised empty hands toward the ceiling.

"He isn't carrying a gun, fella," Clint said. "If you want to try to throw him out, use your hands."

"Bastards got them pig stickers," Errol complained. "If'n he'll get rid of them swords, I'll take him on."

"These swords are my *daisho*," Kaiju stated. "They are the traditional weapons of a samurai. The *katana* or long sword is the soul of a samurai warrior. It has been handed down through my family for generations. I value it more than life. More than your life. More than my own."

"Your backbone is as yellow as your skin, China boy," Errol snickered. "Guess you ain't got the sand to take me on without them big knives."

"Clint-*san*," Kaiju turned to the Gunsmith. "I believe you are a man of honor. Would you guard my daisho, please?"

"I'll look after your swords," Clint replied. "But that fella's a lot bigger than you. Maybe you shouldn't accept his challenge."

"I appreciate your concern, Clint-san," the Japanese smiled. "Do not concern yourself with my safety, please. My swords will be safe, yes?"

"You bet," Clint assured him.

"*Domo arigato,*" Kaiju bowed. "In my language, this is the deepest expression of thanks. There is no English equivalent that I know of, Clint-san."

"You gonna shuck them swords, yellow boy?" Errol demanded as he unbuckled his gunbelt. "You can still run outta here if'n you don't want a whuppin'."

Kaiju took the swords from his sash and carefully placed them on the bar beside the Gunsmith. Then he turned to face the burly cowboy. Errol smiled. He towered at least six inches taller than the samurai, and he outweighed Kaiju by at least sixty pounds.

"All right, China boy," Errol announced. "I'm gonna bust you up."

Kaiju calmly stepped out of his wooden sandals and waited for the cowboy to make the first move. He raised his hands, fingers arched like the claws of an eagle. The Gunsmith had seen similar Oriental fighting styles before. Clint almost felt sorry for Errol.

The big man charged, swinging a mallet-like fist. Kaiju's right leg shot out in a lightning-quick side kick. The edge of his foot slammed into Errol's rib cage. The cowboy groaned and began to double over, but Kaiju suddenly seized Errol's arm and hurled him into the bar.

Errol gasped breathlessly when his spine connected with the counter. Kaiju shouted a war cry and whirled to slash the side of his left hand under Errol's heart. The cowboy half-coughed, half-choked, and folded at the middle. Kaiju's right hand chopped the larger man behind the ear. Errol started to fall, and Kaiju executed a high kick, ramming his heel under his opponent's jaw. The bully crashed to the floor unconscious. Blood oozed from holes in his gums which had formerly contained teeth.

"Son of a bitch!" another cowboy snarled as he raised a chair and attacked the samurai.

Kaiju suddenly took a wide step to the left and moved

out of the path of the descending chair. The furniture struck the floor hard. Two wooden legs snapped on impact. Kaiju stomped a kick to the side of his attacker's knee. The cowboy howled as bone and cartilage crunched in his leg.

The samurai grabbed his opponent's arm, holding the wrist in one hand and the elbow in the other. Kaiju jammed an elbow under the cowboy's armpit. He quickly shuffled his feet to the left, yanked the captive limb over his shoulder, and pulled the arm hard. The cowboy screamed as his shoulder joint popped. The samurai rammed an elbow into the man's breastbone to send him staggering across the room. The cow-poke wilted to the floor, clutching his injured arm.

The fellow who looked like a jackass grabbed a bottle by its neck and prepared to hurl it at Kaiju. Another cowboy pulled his pistol from leather. The Gunsmith's Colt revolver roared twice, the shots tumbling so close together they sounded like a single explosion. The jackass cried out in alarm when a slug shattered the bottle in his fist. The other cowboy bellowed in pain as another bullet tore into his forearm. The 230 grain lead projectile splintered the bone and burst clean through the man's arm. The cowhand dropped his pistol and fell back into his chair, clutching the bullet-smashed limb.

''Holy shit,'' the fifth cowboy gasped, raising his empty hands in surrender.

''I think the fight's over,'' Clint Adams commented as he lowered his modified Colt, ''unless you fellas want to keep it going.''

''You win,'' the jackass said through clenched teeth, trying to pluck shards of broken glass from his bloodied hand. ''Jesus Christ, you're a couple of mean bas— fellers.''

''Just remember who started it,'' the Gunsmith told

him. "Some of your friends need a doctor. Best have their injuries looked after right away, or the doc might have to do some amputations."

"Oh, shit," the man with the wounded arm gasped. "Come on. Let's get outta here."

The cowboys dragged their wounded out the batwings. Clint watched them carefully, leery of sudden tricks to try to catch him off guard. Kaiju returned to the bar and slid his swords into the sash around his waist.

"I thank you again, Clint-san," he declared. "And now I will have my beer. Yes?"

TWO

"I don't think I heard your name well enough to try to pronounce it," the Gunsmith admitted.

"My family name is Kaiju and my given name is Inoshiro," the samurai replied. "Inoshiro is awkward for Americans so you may call me Kaiju, Clint-san."

"Just Clint," the Gunsmith said. "There's no 'son' at the end of it."

"My apologies, Clint," Kaiju began. "Clint-san means 'Mr. Clint'. I used this term to convey my respect for you. I'm afraid I still have some trouble getting used to English."

"You speak English just fine, Kaiju," Clint assured him. "And you sure know how to use your hands and feet. Reminded me of how a couple friends of mine fight. I know two Chinese-American detectives in San Francisco named John Chang and Sam Wing. They called their fighting style *chuan shu*."*

"That is Chinese," Kaiju said, a trace of contempt in his voice. "But we samurai learn far better fighting arts. *Jujutsu* and the Okinawan art of *karate*, which means 'empty hand.' Of course, the main fighting art of the samurai is *kenjutsu*, sword fighting."

"I can't honestly say I know much about samurai,"

_____
Gunsmith #27: Chinatown Hell

13

Clint admitted as he sipped his beer. "But isn't a samurai sort of like a European knight? You serve a king or whatever, and you've got a code of chivalry and all that?"

"There are similarities, Clint," Kaiju nodded. "A samurai's duty is to serve. He serves his *daimyo* warlord as I serve Nagata-*sama*. A samurai is bound by the code of *Bushido* which rules his actions for all things in life."

"That's mighty interestin', Kaiju," Jack the bartender commented as he examined the broken chair and fragments of the shattered beer bottle. "But who's gonna pay for the damage to my place?"

"Hell, Jack," Clint replied. "Those cowboys started it. Make them pay."

"Don't reckon they'll have much money left after Doc Myers finishes patchin' them up," Jack snorted.

"I will pay the damages," Kaiju announced. "That is not a problem."

"It's none of my business, Kaiju," the Gunsmith began, "but I was wondering why a samurai is in a small town in California."

"I am on a mission," Kaiju explained. "A mission for Nagata-sama, my master. I cannot tell you more. I am sorry, Clint."

"No problem," Clint assured him, finishing his beer. "But if you're on a secret assignment, I hate to tell you this, but your clothes don't exactly blend in with everybody else. You're kind of obvious."

"My appearance is not the problem," Kaiju stated. "Besides, I am samurai, and I shall remain samurai. My clothing is traditional. I cannot alter that without a very good reason."

"Yeah," Clint nodded, although he didn't understand what Kaiju meant. "Well, I'm sure you're a fine swordsman, Kaiju, but a sword isn't a match for a gun. You could have gotten your head blown off."

"Life and death are ruled by karma," the samurai declared. "If it is my karma to die by a bullet, I shall accept my fate."

"This karma," the Gunsmith began, "is that sort of like destiny?"

"Hai," Kaiju answered. "Yes, but karma is more personal. It refers to the forces which rule an individual's fate."

"Well," Clint sighed, "I'll tell you what, Kaiju, a forty-five caliber bullet between the eyes is a force which will sure as hell determine your fate permanently."

"Death is not to be feared," Kaiju told him. "To die is to live again. If I die honorably, my next incarnation will be a better life than this. Do you understand?"

"No," the Gunsmith admitted. "But I figure if you have a mission to accomplish, you want to get it done in this lifetime. Right?"

"That is a logical point," Kaiju agreed. "And, in fact, I came into this tavern hoping to find someone who could accompany me on my mission. Someone skilled with firearms. You would be an ideal choice, Clint."

"A mission, huh?" Clint frowned. "I've agreed to a few missions in the past, including one for the president of the United States,* and I can't say as I was real happy with the way most of them turned out."

"This would be an escort duty," Kaiju explained. "Guarding certain valuables on board our train."

"Now, don't take offense by this Kaiju," the Gunsmith began. "But I once hired on as a bodyguard to help escort

---

*Gunsmith #10: New Orleans Fire

a lady from Brownsville, Texas to Yuma, Arizona. Turned out to be something other than what I'd been told. Not one of my happier experiences.* Reckon once bitten, twice shy."

"I think I understand," the samurai assured him. "You do not know me, and you are not familiar with the Japanese culture or samurai. I understand your apprehension, and I do not take offense at your refusal, Clint."

"Thanks," Clint replied. "Finish up your beer, and I'll buy you another."

"No, thank you," Kaiju said. "I should return to the train."

"Good luck with your mission, Kaiju," Clint said. "Whatever it is."

"It may well be my last mission," the samurai said grimly.

"You figure your karma isn't favorable this time?" the Gunsmith asked.

"Death does not worry me, Clint," Kaiju replied. "But it is the future of Nippon—Japan—that concerns me. My country is moving toward the West. It is changing, perhaps too quickly. Our traditions are also changing. Soon there will be no need for samurai. Nippon will have armies with cannons and guns. The way of the sword will become a thing of the past."

"What will you do if that happens?" Clint inquired.

"I do not know," Kaiju confessed. "My father was samurai and his father before him. My ancestors have been samurai for many generations. It is a great and honorable heritage. If it comes to an end, I do not know what I shall do. I shall find out when that time comes."

"Karma?" Clint asked.

"Hai," Kaiju nodded.

---

*Gunsmith #15: Bandit Gold

"What in blue blazin' hell is goin' on in here?" a voice demanded.

Clint turned toward the batwings and saw a pair of men at the threshold. One man appeared to be in his late thirties, with a paunchy belly which hung over his gunbelt. The other was at least ten years younger and carried a Winchester rifle braced against his hip. Both men wore star-shaped badges pinned to their chests.

"Better not head back to the train just yet, Kaiju," the Gunsmith told the samurai. "We've got a Western tradition to take care of first. The law figures they've got a right to know about shootings and brawls and such."

"You can explain what happened," the samurai replied. "I trust you to tell the truth, Clint. You are a man of honor."

"Well, I figure the sheriff will want to hear your side of the story, too," Clint told him. "Let's both talk to him. All right?"

"Very well," Kaiju sighed, already weary of the subject.

"I heard shootin' over here," the sheriff declared as he approached the bar. "And I seen five hired hands from the Double J stumble over to Doc Myers' office. Looked like they been busted up pretty good."

"Indeed," Kaiju announced, "they were lucky to be spared their lives. Is that not true, Clint?"

"Well," the Gunsmith said with a shrug, "I wouldn't say it happened quite like that."

"Then suppose you tell me what did happen, Adams," the lawman suggested, "from the beginning."

THREE

Sheriff Mel Collins listened to the Gunsmith and Kaiju Inoshiro explain what had happened. The lawman propped an elbow against the bar and leaned his chin against the heel of his palm as he fish-eyed Clint Adams and the bizarre Oriental stranger dressed in a fancy robe with two swords sticking out of his belt.

"That's a mighty interestin' story you got there," Collins said after he heard both men speak. "Adams, you got quite a reputation as a gunfighter, but when you rode into town with your gunsmith wagon, you paid me a visit."

"I always like to let the local law know when I'm in their jurisdiction," Clint explained. "Figure you'd want to know about strangers in town, especially one with a reputation."

"You assured me you were in Lawton just to do some gunsmith business," the sheriff remarked. "Fixin' folks broke weapons and such."

"That's a fact, sheriff," the Gunsmith confirmed. "And I wouldn't have gotten involved in this incident if those cowhands had been willing to leave Kaiju be. A big feller named Errol reached for his gun and that's when I stepped in."

"That's purely the way it happened, sheriff," Jack told the lawman. "Errol and the rest of them boys started it. Clint didn't shoot nobody until two of them cowhands

18

tried to jump this Japanese feller from behind. One boy pulled a gun, and the other was gonna throw a bottle. Least I think that's what happened. All took place real fast. I can tell you one thing, sheriff. Ain't never seen such shootin' in all my born days. Clint shot one feller in the arm and busted the bottle in the other jasper's hand quicker than you can bat an eyelash.''

"I didn't figure professional gunmen ever shot anybody just to wound 'em," Collins commented, glaring at the Gunsmith.

"Didn't need to kill them," Clint explained. "Those two cow-pokes were slower than molasses in winter. I could take enough time to aim real careful and just wing 'em. If they'd been faster, maybe I would have had to kill them."

"How about you, stranger?" Collins looked at Kaiju. "You said you put down those swords before you whupped Errol and another cowboy. You ain't very big, feller. I can't imagine you beatin' up a couple of ranch ridin' hellions."

"That little feller can fight, sheriff," Jack announced. "Some sort of fancy Japanese fightin'. Never seen nothin' like it. He bounced big ol' Errol around the place like he was a baby."

"With his bare hands?" Sheriff Collins frowned.

"That is correct, sheriff," Kaiju nodded.

"Then maybe this little pint-sized terror wouldn't mind givin' us a demonstration," the deputy said with a grin as he unbuckled his gunbelt.

"If you insist," the samurai agreed.

"Hold on, Pete," the bartender warned. "You don't know what you're gettin' into."

"Shit," the deputy replied as he launched himself at Kaiju.

The samuari met Pete's lunge. He grabbed the lawman's shirt front with one hand and a sleeve with the other. Kaiju pivoted sharply and hurled Pete over his hip. The deputy crashed to the floor hard. Kaiju stepped back and allowed the young lawman to get to his feet.

Pete wasn't a quitter. He was less reckless as he tried to take on Kaiju again. The deputy jabbed two quick lefts at the samurai's face, but Kaiju easily weaved out of range. Pete then swung a right cross for Kaiju's jaw. The samurai caught the deputy's arm with both hands, whirled suddenly and dropped to one knee.

"Sshhiitt!" Pete howled as his body hurled abruptly through the batwings to land on the plankwalk outside.

"I think you made your point, fella," the sheriff told Kaiju.

"Does that mean you believe us now?" Clint asked dryly.

"I don't figure two men would start a fight with five fellers," Collins replied. "Even if they happen to be two men like you and this Japanese jasper. Reckon those cow-pokes just picked on the wrong two fellers this time. You didn't kill none of 'em, so I can't say you broke the law. Boys probably needed a lesson like this. Might teach 'em not to bully folks in the future."

"Always feels good to do a good deed," the Gunsmith said dryly. "Now, if you don't need me anymore, sheriff, I'd like to get over to the barber shop."

"Just got one question for you and Kaiju here," the lawman replied. "Are you fellas planning to be in town much longer?"

"I'll be leaving Lawton in the morning," Clint assured him.

"I too will leave tomorrow," Kaiju stated. "We have

much distance to travel, and our train has only begun its journey.''

"Good,'' Sheriff Collins declared. ''You fellers ain't really done nothin' wrong, but frankly, I ain't gonna be sorry to see you leave.''

''And here I thought you were gonna offer me the key to the city,'' the Gunsmith said dryly.

FOUR

The Gunsmith left the saloon and crossed the street to the barber shop. He noticed Kaiju heading back toward the train. Clint was intrigued by the samurai and curious about Kaiju's mysterious mission. The Gunsmith mentally told himself that whatever the samurai was involved with, it was none of his business, and he shouldn't get mixed up with it. After all, Kaiju was looking for a gunman. Kaiju wasn't part of a friendly tour of the United States.

However, Kaiju Inoshiro had seemed like a decent man, and Clint suspected the samurai was not unlike himself. The Gunsmith was also part of a rapidly vanishing breed. He was an individualist, a lone drifter who lived pretty much by his own rules. Kaiju was right. The world was changing and there would be less and less room for independence.

Cities were being built in the West. Almost all the Indian territories had been taken over by the white man. Populations were growing and industries from the East would soon start to spread to the West. Civilization. It had little use for individualism.

And, although Clint had never wanted his reputation as the Gunsmith, he was indeed a professional gunfighter. He was one of the last of the great quick-draw artists. Most of the others were already dead. Clint's close friend,

James "Wild Bill" Hickok had been killed a few years earlier. The Gunsmith recalled how Hickok had taken to drinking heavily. Wild Bill's behavior gradually became more confusing, paradoxically adopting an extremely paranoid attitude and yet frequently being quite careless. The latter had eventually cost Hickok his life.*

Perhaps Wild Bill had realized that the old days were coming to an end. Eventually sheriffs and marshalls would be largely replaced by police forces such as those found in the Eastern cities. Even the outlaw gangs were slowly losing ground to organized criminal outfits. Clint had seen evidence of this in New Orleans and San Francisco.† The world was changing, and the future wouldn't have much call for samurai or middle-aged, lightning-fast gunfighters who roamed around the West repairing guns for a living.

"Shit," Clint muttered, annoyed with himself for feeling remorse about a future which might never happen. "Plan for today and maybe tomorrow, but the hell with next year or the year after that."

The Gunsmith entered the barber shop. He noticed the place also offered hot baths for twenty cents. Clint decided to bathe first and get his shave and haircut later. The barber was pleased because he'd make a dollar ten regardless of which order Clint chose to use his services. The owner called his two young sons into the shop and ordered them to prepare a hot bath for his customer.

As Clint soaked in a tub full of steamy water, he pushed aside speculation about Kaiju and his own uncertain future. What mattered most at the present was his dinner date with Alice Walters. The Gunsmith didn't know much about the pretty young lady he met at the general store, but

*Gunsmith #14: Dead Man's Hand
†Gunsmith #23: The Riverboat Gang

she was certainly the most interesting and appealing female he'd encountered in Lawton. Alice also seemed interested in the Gunsmith. This wasn't too surprising since most of the young men in the area seemed to be cowboys from the Double J Ranch. Judging from the five morons Clint had encountered in the saloon, these fellers were more interested in drinking and brawling than women.

Like most men, Clint wondered how the evening would turn out and whether or not Alice would be willing to go to bed with him. The Gunsmith wasn't a hypocrite about sex. He didn't pass moral judgement on a woman who enjoyed sex. Hell, it was the most natural thing in the world—and certainly the most pleasant.

The Gunsmith scrubbed himself with a cake of rather coarse lye-based soap, taking care not to splash water on his gunbelt and clothing which was on a chair next to the tub. He slid down in the water, rinsing his body. Clint sighed as the hot liquid seemed to sink into his muscles, relaxing stiffness and tension.

Without warning, two figures ripped through the canvas tarp nailed to the doorway which served as a screen separating the bathroom from the rest of the barber shop. Clint immediately recognized the pair. They were two of the cowboys he'd encountered in the saloon. The fellow with the jackass features held a .44 Smith & Wesson in his left fist. His right hand was heavily bandaged. The other man's right arm was in a sling, but he had a Remington revolver in his other hand.

"We got you now, you son of a bitch!" the one-armed man snarled.

"Don't look like much without no clothes on," the jackass snickered. "Ain't such a big man now, Mr. Gunsmith."

"Figure you can cripple me for life and then ride outta town and brag 'bout what you done?" the other cowboy snarled. "Think again, Adams."

"I reckon you boys are a might upset with me," Clint commented, trying to sound calmer than he felt.

"You gonna leave this world the way you entered it, Adams," the jackass giggled. "Naked and dripping wet."

"I do admire a man with a sense of irony," the Gunsmith said as he leaned over the tub and reached for the chair. "But you mind if I at least have a cigarette before you kill me?"

"You ain't gettin' nothin', fella," the one-armed man replied as he aimed his gun at Clint, "'cept a funeral."

A shirt draped over the back of the chair concealed Clint's gunbelt from the cowboys' view. They didn't see the Gunsmith draw his modified Colt revolver from its holster. Clint raised the pistol, snap-aimed and triggered the double-action weapon. A .45 bullet burst from the muzzle of the Gunsmith's Colt, crashing into the one-armed man's chest and drilling a lethal tunnel through his heart.

"Christ, no!" the jackass exclaimed as his companion fell back against the doorjamb, blood trickling from his open mouth.

The dying cowboy slumped to the floor as he fired his Smith & Wesson pistol. Clint had already hauled himself over the rim of the bathtub. He heard the report of his opponent's weapon as he dropped to the floor. The gunman's bullet struck the bathwater and punched a hole in the side of the tub.

Clint aimed his Colt and triggered it twice. Two rounds caught the jackass in the solar plexus. The bullets burned upward into the cowhand's chest cavity and ripped into his heart and lungs. The Remington fell from the man's hand as he fell backward through the doorway.

Clint scrambled to his feet. Naked, he darted to the entrance and flattened his back against the wall, taking care to stay clear of the doorway which led to the main room of the barber shop. The Gunsmith hadn't heard the barber or his sons cry out in alarm. This probably meant someone was holding a gun on them.

Clint cautiously moved to the doorway. Water dripped from his naked body. A layer of ice seemed to form along his spine as he prepared to flush the third gunman out.

He leaned toward the doorway and swung an arm over the gap. It was a quick blur of movement which wouldn't expose him to enemy fire, but it might be enough to startle a frightened amateur into pulling a trigger.

The trick worked. A sharp metallic crack of the report of a rifle exploded from the other room. The bullet sizzled through the doorway and smashed into a wall. Clint shuffled to the threshold, both hands wrapped around the grip of his Colt. Errol, the burly cowboy, was busy working the lever action of a Henry carbine.

"Drop it!" the Gunsmith ordered.

Errol jammed the stock-butt of the carbine against a hip and swung the barrel toward Clint. The Gunsmith shot him right between the eyes. The big cow-poke hurtled backward, the Henry still in his fists. He fell against the barber chair and slumped into the seat. Errol's head hung over the back, blood and brains dripping from the exit wound at the back of his skull.

Sheriff Collins burst through the front entrance, pistol in hand. The barber and his sons were huddled in a corner, clinging to each other like frightened bats in a cave. Clint Adams lowered his Colt revolver. Smoke still curled from the muzzle.

"What the hell?" the bewildered lawman began. He glared at the Gunsmith. "Adams, you're naked!"

"Really?" Clint said dryly. "Wondered why it was sort of chilly in here."

"What the hell happened here?" Collins wondered aloud as he stared at Errol's corpse, still sitting in the chair.

"Kind of thing you can expect in a barber shop," the Gunsmith replied with a shrug. "A couple close shaves."

FIVE

Errol and his two companions had been released from the doctor's care. One cowboy was still on his back with a broken leg and a dislocated shoulder. The trio had tried to talk the fifth cowhand into joining them when they tried to get even with Clint Adams and Kaiju Inoshiro, but the fellow had enough sense to refuse. The three vengeful cowhands had then located the Gunsmith and carried out their plan of revenge and murder.

A plan which cost them their lives.

Clint and Sheriff Collins learned the details behind the assassination attempt from the cowboy who had turned down the offer to join the vigilante action. This satisfied the lawman that Clint had acted in self-defense—although the barber had already given testimony to that fact. It also reassured Clint that he wouldn't have to worry about any more Double J hands trying to kill him.

The Gunsmith didn't enjoy killing, but the attackers had left him no choice. Clint didn't have any trouble with his conscience, although the incident had dampened his spirits. Of course, Alice had already heard about the shootings, and she insisted on talking about the subject at the dinner table that night.

"You'd have thought those fools would have learned their lesson after they started trouble in the saloon," she commented as she cut up her steak.

"I guess they figured they had a score to settle with me," the Gunsmith said with a shrug.

"Isn't it scary to be in a gunfight?" Alice inquired.

"Yeah," Clint confirmed. "Nobody likes to be shot at, and nobody in his right mind likes shooting people."

"Does this sort of thing happen very often?" she asked through a forkful of food. "I mean, because you're the Gunsmith?"

"The shooting in the saloon was because I helped Kaiju when those cow-pokes tried to attack him from behind," Clint explained. "It really had nothing to do with the fact some folks call me the Gunsmith. By the way, I'd rather you call me Clint. All right?"

"Oh, sure," Alice agreed. "But doesn't your reputation as a gunfighter cause problems from time to time?"

"My reputation is kind of blown out of proportion," the Gunsmith sighed. "It's all hogwash really. Always was and always will be. Every so often that hogwash causes a problem, but I reckon it could be a lot worse."

"You don't really want to talk about this, do you?" Alice inquired, gazing at Clint with her big blue eyes.

"Not really," he admitted.

"Oh," she frowned. "Sorry."

"That's all right," Clint assured her. "I understand."

The Gunsmith really did understand. Alice Walters was young. Hell, she was about half Clint's age. The young have a lot to learn about life and people. They're curious, and they ask questions. Sometimes these questions are a bit insensitive, but at least their curiosity is honest. It takes years of experience to master insincerity.

Alice was very pretty with curly red hair, a fair complexion, and a compact, shapely figure. Clint tried not to stare at her breasts. The magnificent mounds of flesh strained the fabric of her blue cotton dress. The Gunsmith wasn't quite sure how to make his proposition, but he wanted to go to bed with Alice, and he was leaving in the morning. When one is short on time, one must sometimes be a bit blunt.

"Would you like to see my room?" Clint asked.

"That sounds like a very good idea," the woman replied with a smile.

Thank goodness for the curiosity of youth, the Gunsmith thought.

Clint and Alice left the restaurant and headed for the hotel.

The desk clerk didn't say a word as Clint escorted the young woman up the stairs to his room. She noticed that his hand hovered close to the butt of his holstered revolver as he opened the door.

"Expecting trouble?" Alice whispered.

"I just don't like being caught off guard," he replied. "Expecting trouble is the best way to avoid it from happening."

They entered the room. Clint moved to the table to light the kerosine lamp. Alice told him not to bother.

"I think we can find everything by touch," she remarked.

"Sounds fine to me," the Gunsmith assured her.

He placed his hands on her shoulders and pulled Alice into his arms. Their lips met as they embraced. The kiss was long and full of passion. Alice's fingers quickly moved to his shirt front and began to unfasten the buttons. Clint's hands shifted to her breasts, feeling the nipples harden beneath the cloth.

They helped each other undress in the dark. Clint gradually moved to the bed, guiding Alice to the mattress. He hung his gunbelt on the headboard before he continued to remove his clothing and assist the lady to do likewise.

Alice's skin was warm and smooth with a texture like satin. Her breasts were heavy, the flesh firm and the nipples stiff under Clint's touch. The woman's groping fingers boldly felt his crotch, eagerly stroking his member.

"You're about ready, aren't you?" she whispered, gripping his erection.

"I'll be ready when you are," he promised.

Naked, the couple sprawled out on the mattress. Their hands continued to stroke and fondle. The Gunsmith kissed Alice's breasts. He gently kneaded the nipples with his tongue and teeth. His fingers slid along her belly and slipped between her thighs. Clint's touch moved to her vagina. Alice was already warm and damp.

She found his rigid penis and steered it to her womb. They sighed with pleasure as Clint entered her. He gyrated his hips slowly, working himself deeper. The woman wiggled beneath him, holding onto his neck and shoulders. Alice gasped as he lunged inside her. Her nails dug into his skin as Clint pumped his manhood again and again.

The Gunsmith gradually increased the tempo of his thrusts until Alice cried out in ecstasy. Clint waited for a minute or two before he started grinding and lunging again. This time both lovers reached the summit of passion together. Alice convulsed in another electric orgasm as Clint's swollen member released its seed.

"God, that was good," Alice whispered as she snuggled against Clint's warm body. "Sure wish you weren't leaving in the morning."

"Kind of wish I wasn't going," the Gunsmith replied. "But I've wrapped up my business in Lawton, and I gotta be moving on."

"You sure about that?" she asked, kissing his neck.

"Look, honey," Clint began. "I'm not the sort to settle down and raise a family. That damn-fool 'Gunsmith reputation' would always catch up with me sooner or later. Young gunhawks still try to goad me into a fight from time to time."

"I guess it was a silly idea," Alice sighed.

"Not at all," he assured her. "I'm flattered."

Then the tender moment was interrupted by the sound of gunfire outside the hotel.

"Oh, shit," the Gunsmith muttered. "Now what?"

SIX

Alice groaned with disappointment when Clint extracted himself from the center of her womanhood. The Gunsmith drew his Colt from leather as he climbed out of the bed. Clint crept to the window and peered at the street below.

More gunshots erupted. Clint saw streaks of orange flame at the south end of town. The shooting was taking place at the railroad tracks.

"The train is under attack," the Gunsmith declared. "Kaiju doesn't carry a gun. I'd better check this out."

"Clint," Alice began, concern in her voice, "don't get involved in whatever those Japs are up to. Law and order in Lawton isn't your problem. Let the sheriff handle it."

"I don't have a hell of a lot of faith in Sheriff Collins' ability to handle a small-scale war. That's a hell of a fight going on by the train. I can't just hide under a blanket when something like this is happening."

Clint hastily pulled on his trousers and boots. He didn't bother donning a shirt, but he draped his gunbelt over a shoulder as he hurried to the door. Clint dashed from the room and bounded down the stairs, leaping them three or four steps at a time. He reached the lobby and bolted out the front door.

The cool, night air struck his naked chest like a clammy blanket. He noticed several people gazed out their win-

33

dows at the gun battle taking place at the train, but none of them felt obliged to get involved. More evidence of big-city civilization, the Gunsmith thought with contempt. Don't stick your neck out for anybody else.

Clint jogged along the plankwalk, taking advantage of the dense shadows for cover. He noticed a figure sprawled in front of the sheriff's office. Clint approached quickly and stared down at the motionless shape.

Sheriff Collins lay on his back, the slender shaft of an arrow jutting from the lawman's chest. Clint was startled by the size of the arrow. It was almost four feet long, twice as long as any arrow used by any Indian tribe the Gunsmith was familiar with. Whoever the archer had been, the fellow sure was accurate with a bow. The arrow had struck Collins dead-center in the heart.

"Jesus," the Gunsmith whispered as he glanced about, half-expecting to see a lunatic with a bow and arrow pointed at him, "what am I getting myself into?"

Clint continued to approach the railroad tracks, moving even more cautiously than before. He heard screams of agony as well as gunshots as he drew closer to the train. Figures darted about the tracks, but Clint couldn't see them clearly.

A sixth sense, developed by years of experience at staying alive when a lot of people wanted him dead, alerted Clint to danger. He instinctively dropped to the plankwalk even before he heard the harsh whistle of a projectile cutting through the night air. Clint heard the thud of an object striking the wall of the general store above him. He glanced up and saw the quivering shaft of another long arrow, jutting from the building.

The Gunsmith scurried to his feet and ran to the alley between the store and the local cafe. He dashed into the gap as another arrow sizzled past his running form. Clint wasn't sure where the missile landed. It missed him and that was good enough for Clint.

"Shit," the Gunsmith growled breathlessly, trying to locate the enemy bowman. Of course, a bow and arrow is virtually silent, and it doesn't produce a tell-tale muzzle flash. "Where is the bastard?"

Clint decided to move to the end of the alley and approach the train from the rear. He turned and started to creep forward. Clint almost tripped over the body which lay in the shadows.

The Gunsmith stumbled and fell to one knee beside the corpse. It was Pete, the deputy. His throat had been cut, from ear to ear, by someone who knew his deadly trade very well. The cut was deep, and it severed both carotid and jugular. Pete's shirt was covered with blood. The stains were drying which suggested the corpse had been lying there for more than an hour.

Poor bastard must have been making his rounds when the killer jumped him, Clint thought, as his stomach knotted up. They must have killed him before they attacked the train.

The Gunsmith reached the end of the alley and moved behind the cafe. Then he sprinted six yards to the livery stable. Another arrow hissed as it shot past him so close it seemed to tug at the hair on the back of his neck. Clint dove forward and tucked his head as his shoulder hit the ground. He rolled to the livery, relieved to be behind the cover of the large wooden structure.

He finally reached a position close to the rear of the train. He leaned around the corner and gazed at the caboose. A man with a rifle was squatted on the roof by the cupola. A bandanna was tied around his nose and mouth. Another gunman stood at the rear of the caboose, aiming a six-gun at the windows of a passenger car.

"Hold it!" the Gunsmith shouted.

Both gunmen whirled, weapons swinging toward Clint. The Gunsmith's modified Colt snarled. The man on the roof of the caboose screamed as a .45 bullet crashed into his chest. He tumbled backward and fell off the caboose. A cloud of dust rose when his body crashed to the ground.

The other gunman snapped off a hasty shot at the Gunsmith. A bullet splintered wood from the corner of the livery. Clint ignored it and aimed carefully before squeezing the trigger of his Colt revolver. The gunman's head bounced as a .45 slug ripped through it. The stetson popped off his shattered skull as he collapsed in a lifeless heap.

The Gunsmith dashed forward to the caboose. He noticed two or three more figures along the side of the train as well as a couple more bodies sprawled on the ground. Someone shouted something in a language Clint didn't understand. Another voice cursed in English. The Gunsmith peered around the corner and saw two rifle-toting figures charge toward him. Clint prepared to aim his Colt at the pair.

Suddenly, one of the gunmen screamed and fell forward. He landed on his face, a long arrow shaft protruding from between his shoulder blades. The other rifleman whirled and fired his weapon at a passenger window. The bullet shattered glass, but Clint wasn't sure if the gunman shot his intended target. The man turned his attention back to Clint.

The Gunsmith triggered his double-action Colt twice. Both slugs struck the gunman in the chest. The impact lifted him off his feet and hurled the gunhawk four feet before he crashed to the ground—dead. Clint didn't see any further immediate threat at that side of the train. He turned to the opposite side.

A ribbon of steel flashed from the darkness. Clint retreated from the slashing blade. He nearly stumbled and instinctively moved in that direction because it was the quickest way to dodge the attacking steel. The Gunsmith fell on his back and raised his Colt as a shape dressed entirely in black stood over him with a sword held in a two-hand grip.

Clint had encountered a lot of strange opponents in the past. But he had never seen an adversary like the black-clad swordsman. The man looked like a shadow. His head and face were covered with black cloth and only his eyes were visible. He wore strange gloves which covered the palm and back of his hands, but not the fingers. His feet were clad in odd black slippers which divided the big toe from the rest of his toes.

The Gunsmith observed all of this with a single glance. The swordsman didn't give him time for a better look. The killer raised his weapon and prepared to use the blade once more. The Gunsmith quickly pointed his Colt at the attacker and squeezed the trigger as fast as he could.

Two bullets slammed into the swordsman's masked face. His head snapped back, and the sword fell from open fingers. The man in black fell to one knee, blood oozing from his bullet-crushed features. Then he melted to the ground without uttering a sound.

Clint rolled over and got to his feet. His fingers trembled as he opened the loading gate of his pistol and extracted the spent shell casings. The Gunsmith breathed deeply through his nose and out his mouth, trying to calm his rattled nerves. Clint's hands were steady as he began to reload his weapon.

Suddenly, another black shape materialized from the shadows. Clint wasn't even sure where the bastard had come from. He just blinked, and the assassin appeared.

The Gunsmith closed the loading gate and tried to turn the cylinder in order to get a live round under the firing pin.

Something struck his wrist, knocking the pistol from Clint's hand. A sharp blow to the midsection drove the wind out of the Gunsmith's lungs. Christ, Clint thought. What the hell is this jasper hitting me with?

The Gunsmith saw a blur of motion and raised a forearm to protect his head, hoping that his arm wouldn't be chopped in two. A hard object struck the limb, sending shards of pain along nerves up to his shoulder. Clint finally realized what his opponent's weapon was. The attacker was armed with a black stave which was almost invisible in the dark.

Clint lunged forward and swung a fist into his opponent's face. The punch was solid, and the man in black was spun around by the blow. Or maybe he simply pivoted with the motion, because the assailant whirled and unleashed a spinning side kick to the Gunsmith's abdomen.

Clint doubled over with a gasp. The attacker spun about again and slashed his pole at the Gunsmith. Clint turned sharply and caught the stave in both hands. He tried to pull his opponent off balance, but the man in black moved with the motion and lashed a foot in a high roundhouse kick.

The Gunsmith's head seemed to explode when the kick connected with the side of his skull. Lights burst painfully inside his head, but Clint held onto the stave. His opponent did not do likewise. The man released the stick and suddenly jumped back.

Clint saw the man in black reach for the hilt of a sword thrust in a black sash. Steel flashed as the assassin drew his weapon. The Gunsmith weaved on unsteady legs, his vision already blurred by the punishment he'd received in the fight. Clint still held the black stave in his hands, but that seemed a feeble weapon against the lethal assailant's sword.

"Haaii!" a voice screamed in fury.

Kaiju Inoshiro charged forward, his katana long sword in his fists. The man in black met the samurai's attack and swung his sword at Kaiju. The samurai blocked the other man's weapon with the flat of his sword.

Kaiju suddenly whirled like a top. His katana cut with the motion and slashed the aggressor across the chest. The samurai raised his weapon overhead as he completed the turn to once again face the wounded man. Kaiju swung the sword and sliced a deep diagonal cut in his opponent's upper chest. The terrible wound extended from the man's collarbone to his solar plexus. The man in black slumped to the ground. His body trembled slightly before it surrendered to the final judgement of death.

"Clint-san!" the samurai exclaimed as he turned to the Gunsmith. "Are you injured, my friend?"

"I don't think so," Clint assured him. "I'm sure as hell better off than I would have been if you hadn't showed up when you did."

"But you did not do badly on your own, Clint," the samurai declared, looking down at the other corpses which littered the ground.

"Looks like the battle is over now," the Gunsmith commented. "Mind telling me what it was all about?"

"I would like to confide in you, Clint," Kaiju replied. "But I am not certain if my master would approve."

"Do not worry, Kaiju-san," a voice announced.

Clint turned to see a stout, bald-headed man dressed in a red robe similar to Kaiju's garment. He bowed at the Gunsmith as he stepped onto the platform of the caboose.

"I believe Mr. Adams deserves some answers to his questions," the man declared. "Please, come with me, Mr. Adams. I'll explain everything to you, sir."

SEVEN

"Allow me to introduce myself," the bald man began as he ushered Clint Adams aboard the train. "I am Nagata Hido, daimyo warlord under his imperial majesty, the emperor of Nippon."

"Pleased to meet you," Clint replied. "But I'm not quite sure what to call you, sir. From what little I know about Japanese royalty, a fella has to be careful not to be offensive unless he wants a samurai to cut his head off."

"Just call me Mr. Nagata," the warlord assured him. "I promise not to take offense. We Japanese are, after all, visitors in your country. As guests, we must try to conform to your customs and code of conduct. However, I am very pleased that you had the good manners to consider our customs as well, Mr. Adams."

"I figure it's your train, Mr. Nagata," the Gunsmith said. "Of course, this little battle took place at the town of Lawton, and the folks here might be a bit upset about it. Especially since the sheriff and his deputy were both killed."

"Are you sure of this, Mr. Adams?" Nagata inquired, his bushy eyebrows knitting as he frowned.

"I saw their bodies," Clint confirmed. "The sheriff had been shot in the heart by an arrow, and the deputy's throat was cut. Figure your attackers didn't want them to interfere."

40

"That is most distressing, Mr. Adams," the warlord said, shaking his head sadly. "After we speak, I must talk to the leader of this town. That would be the mayor, correct?"

"I guess so," Clint said with a shrug. "I don't know if they have a mayor here or not. Some of these little towns out here are kind of thrown together. Still, I imagine they've got a mayor in Lawton."

Kaiju addressed Nagata in Japanese, humbly bowing before his warlord. The samurai spoke rapidly in Japanese. Nagata replied in the same language. Kaiju bowed again and hurried outside.

"Apparently the *ninja* and their American allies have retreated," Nagata explained to Clint. "Kaiju and some of my other samurai are going to make certain the attack is really over. One cannot be too careful when dealing with ninja."

"Ninja?" the Gunsmith asked. "What exactly are ninja?"

"I will explain everything," Nagata promised. "Please have patience, Mr. Adams."

The Gunsmith followed the Japanese warlord as he crossed over to the stock car linked to the caboose. The cattle car was remarkably clean. It resembled a miniature stable, containing ten separate stalls with horses. The animals appeared to be well fed and cared for. The floor had been recently swept, and the walls of the car weren't stained with soot, probably due to the fact it was further away from the engine than most cattle cars.

"We will enter the passenger compartments next," Nagata announced. "The floors are covered with *tatamai* mats. Please, remove your shoes before entering, Mr. Adams."

"All right," the Gunsmith agreed, surprised by the request.

When he stepped inside the passenger car, Clint understood why Nagata had asked him to remove his footgear. The floor was covered by numerous square-shaped mats, placed together like tiles. The tatamai appeared to be made of woven reeds which would have been damaged by Clint's boots. Nagata placed his wooden sandals in a corner and Clint followed.

The Gunsmith felt as if he had just entered a foreign country. The compartment sure as hell didn't resemble any passenger car he'd ever been inside before. There were no seats. The only furniture seemed to be some tables with stubby little legs. There were several wooden chests neatly lined up by the walls, and several tall ornate paper screens which separated a series of mattresses that lay flat on the floor.

"These quarters belong to my samurai," Nagata explained. "The screens grant each man some degree of privacy. Japan is a very crowded country. We have many people and privacy is most precious to our people."

"Makes sense," Clint agreed.

"Without privacy one can go mad, Mr. Adams," Nagata declared. "Long ago, my people learned that sometimes the only way to attain privacy is to retreat into one's own mind. We do this through meditation and through rituals. Many of our rituals are handed down by tradition. These often serve to instruct without written word, but they also give our people time to contemplate actions as they relate to each individual personally. Other rituals are a private matter, created by the individual."

"I guess everybody does something like that," Clint remarked. "I just never thought of it as rituals before."

"Perhaps such private actions are really just eccentric

habits," Nagata smiled. "But I prefer to think of them as rituals. We Japanese fancy mystical concepts. Please try to bear with me in this, Mr. Adams."

Nagata led Clint to another passenger car. It was similar to the samurai quarters, but the furnishings were far more impressive. Teak cabinets with jeweled handles, oil lamps mounted on golden dragon statues, and delicate ivory figures on ebony pedestals labeled the quarters as the property of a wealthy man.

"I take it you stay here," the Gunsmith assumed.

"Indeed," Nagata nodded. "Please be seated, Mr. Adams."

Clint didn't see a chair so he lowered himself to the floor and sat cross-legged as he would in an Indian tipi. Two stern-faced young men carrying the long and short swords stood guard beside a rice paper screen. They watched Clint with suspicion, their hands poised on the handles of their fighting swords.

Nagata spoke to the samurai in their native language. The guards bowed to the Gunsmith. One man turned and walked to a chest. He opened it and extracted a robe. The samurai knelt before Clint Adams, offering the garment as he held his head low.

"*Dozo*, Adam-san," the man urged.

"It is not proper to be bare-chested in a man's home, Mr. Adams," Nagata explained. "Of course, you did not plan this visit, so you have not offended me, but please, accept this *kimono* as a gift of friendship and gratitude."

"Thank you," Clint said, accepting the robe. He tried to recall what Kaiju had said in the saloon earlier that day. "*Domo arigato*."

The samurai looked at Clint with surprise and nodded eagerly. "*Do itashi-mahite*, Adam-san," he declared.

The Gunsmith examined the kimono. It was made of

fine silk, royal blue with bright yellow characters similar to Chinese ideographs. Clint donned the robe and tied a cloth sash around his waist to hold it together. Nagata nodded with approval.

"And now," the warlord began, "I must explain why we are in the United States and why the ninja and their American henchmen attacked this train. You are aware that your country and Japan have been exchanging limited trade since Admiral Perry traveled to Nippon in the year 1853?"

"Yeah," Clint replied. "From what I understood Japan has always been sort of an isolationist country which hasn't been too eager to get too close with American trade. Of course, the United States is traditionally an isolationist nation, too. A lot of Americans are afraid we'll get close diplomatic ties to other countries and then if those countries get into a war they'll drag the United States into it as well."

"Indeed," Nagata nodded. "Many Japanese share this concern. Of course, the first Westerners who established relations with Nippon were the Portuguese. They proved to be more interested in exploiting us than trading fairly. The Portuguese sent their missionaries to try to convert us, their traders to try to cheat us, and their diplomats to try to woo Japan into assisting them in a European war which was none of our concern."

"I can see why the Japanese would be sort of suspicious of Westerners after that," Clint agreed. "But I seem to recall that America had an embassy in Japan, and it was attacked to protest our forming relations with your country."

"This is true," Nagata confirmed. "That incident caused much distrust and lack of cooperation between our countries. That is why the emperor has sent me to deliver a gift of friendship and admiration to your president in Washington D.C.''

"A gift?" Clint raised his eyebrows.

Nagata uttered a curt order in Japanese. One of the samurai moved to the screen and pulled it aside to reveal a magnificent gold statue of a figure clad in armor plates with a horned helmet on his proud head. The warrior was mounted on a stout horse, also decked with engraved armor. The base of the statue was wide and etched with numerous ideographs. The entire figure stood a foot and a half tall. It appeared to be made of solid gold which reflected the lamp light. Shards of light danced along the metal figure as if it possessed an electrical life of its own.

''This is the *Horseman of Edo*,'' Nagata explained. ''It was created by the great metalsmith and artist Yumio Itoh in the thirteenth century. It symbolizes the strength of Japan and her great city of Edo. The samurai on horseback is defending his city, protecting the peace. He is not aggressive or arrogant, but proud of his country and devoted to his noble duties.''

''I can see that in the sculpture,'' Clint told Nagata. ''It's really beautiful, Mr. Nagata.''

''And very valuable, Mr. Adams,'' the warlord stated. ''The gold alone is worth a fortune, but the value as an art object symbolic of the very soul of Japan makes it beyond price.''

''Well, the gold could have attracted those outlaws who attacked the train tonight,'' Clint began. ''But those fellas dressed in black with the swords were Japanese, right?''

''Ninja,'' Nagata nodded. ''Professional espionage agents and assassins. They are products of the lower classes of Japan. Each ninja clan is ruled by a leader called a *jonin*. He is hired, usually by a daimyo, to supply agents or *genin* to carry out certain covert actions. Someone has obviously hired a ninja clan to stop the *Horseman of Edo* from being delivered to your president.''

"But how did these ninja wind up in America?" the Gunsmith inquired.

"They must have been sent on another ship from Japan before we arrived," Nagata explained. "The genin agents are probably accompanied by a *chunin* or unit chief to coordinate the mission. They obviously realized they could not operate in this country alone, so they enlisted the outlaws as you call them.''

"I think I understand why Kaiju wanted to hire me to ride shotgun on the train," Clint commented. "Was this the first time the train has been attacked?"

"Yes," Nagata confirmed. "But I feared something like this might happen. Hedora was violently opposed to giving away the *Horseman*. I am certain he is responsible for this.''

"All right," Clint sighed. "Now who the hell is Hedora?''

"Excuse me, Mr. Adams," Nagata said. "I forget that you are unfamiliar with Japan or the ruling classes of Edo and Yedo. Hedora Fumi is a daimyo, like myself, but very much opposed to trade with the West. He does not want Japan to change. He fears that association with Europeans and Americans will corrupt Nippon and ruin our traditional way of life.''

"But you're going to continue to transport the *Horseman* to Washington D.C.?" the Gunsmith asked. "You know you'll have to travel clear to the opposite side of the country. That's one hell of a long trip and a lot can happen between here and Washington. Of course, you may have wiped out all the ninja and enemy gunmen tonight, but I wouldn't count on that if I was you.''

"I am sure we haven't seen the last of the ninja,''

Nagata said grimly. "No chunin would have sent his entire force of genin agents to attack a single target without knowing the full strength of his opponents. The nature of the ninja is that of stealth and cunning, not direct attack. The ninja will attack again. They are the most cunning of opponents. Very dangerous, very resourceful. Ninja are masters of invisibility and destruction. Three of my samurai were killed in the battle tonight. I fear more shall perish before we reach our destination."

"I don't know anything about these ninja characters except those two bastards who attacked me were as quiet as Apaches and tougher than cornered cougars. You'll have enough trouble with those fellas, but you'll have even less of a chance against professional gunmen. These samurai might be the best sword fighters in the world, but a man with a gun doesn't have to get close to kill somebody. A sword against a gun isn't a fair fight, regardless of how good your samurai warrior is."

"What you say might be true, Mr. Adams," Nagata admitted. "But I cannot abandon my mission. It is a matter of honor. I am bound by the code of Bushido to follow the orders of my emperor. Even if it costs my life and the lives of all my samurai."

"Sure one hell of a mess you fellas got," the Gunsmith sighed. "Tell me, Mr. Nagata, are you still interested in hiring me to accompany this train across country?"

"You would agree to take such risks, Mr. Adams?" the warlord asked, startled by Clint's question.

"I didn't know what you fellas were up to before and I didn't know what kind of odds you were up against," Clint explained. "Reckon I just can't let you go on by yourselves and not have to worry about my conscience bothering me later. Might say that's part of *my* code of honor."

"We would indeed be pleased and honored if you would accompany us, Mr. Adams," Nagata assured him. "And, of course, you will be paid well for your trouble."

"Accepting money isn't against my code of honor," the Gunsmith said with a grin. "But I reckon we've got a few things to take care of before we leave. Better look into that right now."

"I admire a man who is practical as well as courageous," Nagata said with a bow.

How do you feel about fellas who are just plain damn fools? Clint thought, but all he said was, "Thank you."

EIGHT

The Gunsmith and Nagata met with the mayor of Lawton and explained what had happened. The mayor wasn't happy about the fact Sheriff Collins and his deputy were murdered by ninja assassins because of the Japanese delegation on the train.

"Well," the Gunsmith commented, "maybe this wouldn't have happened if everybody in town hadn't hidden under their bed when there was trouble. Or, do you really think two lawmen should have had to take on a gun battle without any support from the people of Lawton?"

The mayor didn't have an answer for that question, but he didn't like it either. However, he was glad when Nagata assured him the train would be leaving in the morning, and the Gunsmith would be going with them.

Clint returned to his hotel room. Alice Walters was relieved that he had not been harmed. The couple went back to bed. Alice didn't ask any questions, which the Gunsmith was thankful for. They made love one more time and drifted into a peaceful, sound sleep.

When Clint awoke in the morning, Alice was already gone. He dressed, gathered up his saddlebags and Springfield carbine, and left the room. The Gunsmith descended the stairs. The timid desk clerk was on duty once more. He seemed even more frightened of Clint Adams than he had been the day before.

"Good morning," Clint greeted. "How you doing today?"

"Fine, Mr. Adams," the clerk replied nervously. "Are you leaving today, sir?"

"Yeah," the Gunsmith said with a shrug. "Reckon good news travels fast. Do you want me to sign out or anything?"

"Uh . . . no need for that, Mr. Adams," the desk clerk assured him. "Everything is taken care of, sir."

"Then I'll be on my way," Clint told him.

The Gunsmith headed for the livery stable. The hostler was probably the only person in Lawton other than Alice who would be sorry to see Clint leave town. The Gunsmith had paid the liveryman extra to look after his wagon, team horses, and Duke. He was especially concerned about his prized Arabian gelding and insisted that Duke always got the very best of care. However, now it was time for Clint to be moving on.

He hitched the wagon to the team and tied Duke to a guideline at the rear of the rig. Clint drove the wagon to the train where Nagata and his samurai awaited his return. The Gunsmith had explained that he had to transport his wagon and animals. The Japanese had promised to make room on the train for Clint's belongings.

They placed ramps against the opening of a cattle car and another compartment which had been converted to haul cargo. Clint's team horses calmly marched up the ramp to the cattle car, but Duke backed away, neighed in protest and shook his head hard. Two of the samurai approached with ropes, but Clint waved them away.

"Stay back," the Gunsmith instructed. "I'll take care of Duke. Just let me talk to him for a minute."

Kaiju Inoshiro translated the Gunsmith's remark for the benefit of the other two samurai. They seemed surprised and asked Kaiju a question in Japanese. Clint later learned the pair had asked Kaiju if he was certain he understood what the American had said.

"Hai," Kaiju confirmed with a stern nod.

Clint approached Duke. The horse snorted angrily at the Gunsmith and turned his head aside. Clint stepped closer and patted Duke on the neck.

"Come on, big fella," the Gunsmith urged. "It won't be so bad. They've really got a nice setup inside."

Duke snorted again and pawed the ground with a forehoof. The Gunsmith rolled his eyes.

"Look," he began, "I know you hate trains, but they've got regular stables in there. It won't be like that other long trip we made across country from Texas to Arizona.* I know that trip was hard on you, and the cattle car was all dirty and sooty, but this time will be different."

Duke still pawed the ground. Clint scratched the gelding's muzzle. Duke turned a large dark eye toward the Gunsmith and blinked as if trying to evaluate his owner's honesty.

"Trust me," Clint urged.

The horse snorted again, still not convinced. However, he allowed Clint to take his reins and followed him up the ramp. When the gelding saw the clean interior of the cattle car, his attitude immediately improved. Duke neighed happily and bobbed his head as if agreeing to Clint's demands willingly.

"There," the Gunsmith smiled as Duke rubbed his snout against Clint's chest. "What'd I tell you?"

The samurai watched with astonishment and whispered something to Kaiju. The commander of the samurai unit

---

*Gunsmith #15: Bandit Gold

laughed and shook his head. Clint asked what was so funny.

"They think you are a magician," Kaiju explained. "You have bewitched your horse, or perhaps you bewitched a man and turned him into a horse. Which is it, Clint?"

"That'll be my secret," the Gunsmith said dryly. "Let's get my wagon on board. I'm afraid I haven't learned how to cast any spells on it, so we'll just have to push it."

"Do not feel badly, Clint," Kaiju remarked. "The only magic you'll need will be your sorcery with a gun."

NINE

The train left Lawton before noon. Clint Adams stood at the platform of the caboose, leaning against the handrail as he watched the town fade from view. He didn't feel any great longing to get a final look at Lawton, but he did want to see if anyone was following the train on horseback.

Clint's actions were just a precaution. He didn't really expect to see ninja on horseback galloping along behind them. If Nagata's theory was correct, the ninja killers had already been in the United States before the Japanese delegation with the *Horseman of Edo* arrived. That meant the shadowy men in black had had plenty of time to get organized and plan their strategy. The train would only be heading one way and the ninja knew the destination. They wouldn't be dragging ass trying to catch up with the train. They'd already be ahead of the delegation, planning some sort of ambush.

The outlaws hired by the ninja might be the greater threat, but Clint Adams was familiar with their breed. Most outlaws and gunmen were just plain dumb. They weren't bright enough to learn a trade and too lazy to work, so they'd join forces like a pack of retarded wolves to loot and steal. They usually didn't steal enough to make their efforts worthwhile. When they did get a large bundle

53

of cash, outlaws usually spent it all on gambling, whorehouses, and liquor.

Only a few bank robbers or train robbers were clever. Some of these made a nice sum of money, but most were tripped up by the morons they were forced to work with. Clint doubted that the ninja could have hired any real professionals. That meant the outlaws who would take a job like this would be the usual bottom-of-the-barrel halfwits.

Of course, they didn't need sharp professionals. Any damn fool can point a gun and shoot. The Gunsmith was riding with a bunch of samurai who didn't even own any guns, let alone know how to use them. Swords were no match for even ten rifles at a hundred yards, and even the Gunsmith wasn't good enough to take on an entire gang single-handed.

He turned to walk into the caboose. Clint stopped abruptly, surprised to find himself gazing into the face of one of the most beautiful women he had ever met. She was Japanese, petite, and shapely. Even the loose-fitting blue and white kimono she wore could not conceal the fullness of her breasts. The woman's face was oval-shaped with large dark eyes, a delicate nose and a wide, full mouth. Her raven black hair was fashioned in a bun and held together by a silver pin with a pearl head.

"Excuse me, Mr. Adams," she said in a gentle voice which reminded the Gunsmith of the music of singing birds at early morning. "I did not mean to startle you."

"No problem, ma'am," Clint assured her. "I just didn't know anybody was back there."

"A woman does well to walk softly, Mr. Adams," she smiled. "Men prefer women to be silent, yes?"

"I wouldn't say that," the Gunsmith replied with a

grin. "I've found many beautiful ladies to have a great deal of value to talk about. And your beauty rivals any that I have ever met, ma'am."

The young woman laughed. "Ah, such charm and flattery. I have always heard that Americans were a bit coarse with women, but you speak with the silvered tongue of a European adventurer, Mr. Adams."

"I just see your beauty and speak honestly, ma'am," Clint told her. "Unfortunately, I don't know your name. Is it proper for me to ask you directly or does someone have to introduce us?"

"My name is Rikko," she replied, bowing slightly. "I am Nagata-sama's daughter."

"Oh," Clint nodded, a little disappointed that the lovely lady was the boss's daughter. "Pleased to meet you, Miss Nagata."

"Please call me Rikko, Mr. Adams," she urged.

"Only if you call me Clint," he answered.

"Very well," Rikko agreed. "You seem troubled, Clint. May I ask what is wrong?"

"Just thinking about this little trip across country," the Gunsmith explained. "There's going to be plenty of opportunity for the enemy to attack this train between here and Washington, D.C."

"If that is to be, it shall be," Rikko stated. "That is karma, yes?"

"Maybe," Clint replied. "But I don't see any reason to tempt fate if you don't have to. Transporting a golden statue worth a fortune from one end of the United States to the other is mighty risky. Especially when it's being guarded by just half a dozen fellas with swords and one jasper with an exaggerated reputation as a master gunfighter."

"My father tells me you killed four men in combat last night," Rikko commented. "I would not say your skills are exaggerated, Clint."

"Did he also tell you I almost got my head chopped off by one of those ninja characters?" Clint snorted.

"There is no dishonor in this," Rikko assured him. "The ninja are the most dangerous and cunning of foes. The samurai speak of them with contempt because the ninja come from a lower social level than the samurai, but do not believe the claims that ninja are cowards or poor fighters. The samurai say this because of prejudice, not fact. In truth, the ninja have been trained since childhood, and they are probably as skilled in the ways of combat as the samurai."

"Well, Kaiju didn't seem to have much trouble taking on the ninja who was about to split me in two," Clint remarked.

"Kaiju-san is my father's samurai captain," Rikko explained. "He is the finest swordsman of my father's rentai. Very few ninja or samurai can equal Kaiju-san's skill with a sword. Father has said that of all samurai he has ever known, Kaiju-san is the most remarkable. He has always upheld the code of Bushido and he has always worked harder to master the skills of the samurai. It will be very difficult for Kaiju-san to put up his swords when he returns to Japan."

"Kaiju said the emperor planned to sort of phase out the samurai," Clint frowned. "The idea depressed him."

"Actually, the samurai class was dissolved in 1868," Rikko sighed. "They may no longer carry their swords in public and many of their rights and privileges have been terminated. Kaiju carries his swords now because this is his mission. It will almost certainly be his last."

"And he knows it," Clint said. "That must be pretty hard on him."

"Indeed," Rikko confirmed. "How would you feel if you were no longer allowed to carry your pistol, Clint?"

"I don't think I'd obey a law like that," the Gunsmith admitted. "I'd probably move to another state or even another country if I had to."

"But you are an American," she said. "You are not Japanese, and you are not samurai. Kaiju would never disobey an order. His place in life is to serve his daimyo. He will agree to these conditions when he returns to Japan, regardless of how much it grieves him."

"But Kaiju said that his katana—I think that's what he called the long sword—is the soul of his family," the Gunsmith stated. "If he's being told he can't carry his sword anymore, isn't that sort of like telling him he has to leave his soul at home?"

"The emperor may even order the samurai to surrender their swords," Rikko said sadly. "If that happens, I doubt that Kaiju will be able to live with the shame. The code of Bushido means he must obey orders, but it also states that a samurai must always have his katana. Without it, he has no soul, no purpose. He becomes nothing. I fear Kaiju would choose *seppuku* rather than dishonor either portion of the code he lives by."

"Oh, boy," Clint muttered. "What's seppuku? Japanese for suicide?"

"A very special form of ritual suicide," Rikko explained. "The subject disembowels himself by cutting open his lower abdomen with a knife or short sword. A second may then end his suffering by decapitation."

"Jesus," the Gunsmith rasped. "You really think he'd do that?"

"It is an honorable death, Clint," Rikko declared. "In fact, if we fail in our mission here in America, every one of us is prepared to commit suicide rather than fail our emperor."

"You mean you're really willing to cut your guts out rather than return to Japan without delivering the *Horseman of Edo* to the president?" Clint frowned.

"I will not have to disembowel myself," Rikko explained. "I am a woman so I would commit seppuku by cutting my throat."

"I suppose you'll all say it's karma and then you'll get out your knives and start cutting, huh?" Clint said with disgust. "Damn silly waste of life, if you ask me."

"It is our way, Clint," Rikko smiled gently. "I do not expect you to understand. I do not understand all of our traditions myself. But it is better to die with honor than live in disgrace. Our honor depends on delivering the *Horseman* to your American president. If we cannot accomplish this mission, then we will do what we must to restore our honor. Do you understand now?"

"No," Clint confessed, "and I don't think this train ride is going to be long enough for me to learn enough about you Japanese to understand this sort of thing. But it sure gives me another good reason to help you folks get that statue to Washington. I sure don't want to have to watch all of you kill yourselves."

He pointed a finger at Rikko's neck.

"Besides," Clint commented, "that throat is much too pretty for you to cut it open with a knife."

"I will do what honor dictates, Clint," Rikko smiled. "But thank you for the compliment and your concern for my well being. It is not necessary, however. What will happen will happen."

"Yeah," the Gunsmith shrugged. "Well, I think I'll have a talk with your father and see if I can't convince him to agree to a couple things which might tilt the scales of karma in our favor."

TEN

"I have a suggestion about our little trip, Mr. Nagata," Clint Adams began when he found the Japanese warlord in his quarters. "May I state my ideas?"

"Please do, Mr. Adams," Nagata invited as he knelt on the tatamai-covered floor, writing *kan-ji* ideographs on a sheet of parchment with a whale bone writing brush tipped with horsehair.

"Look," the Gunsmith began, "we're going to cross the California border into the Arizona Territory. When we do, let's take my wagon, load the *Horseman of Edo* on it and take the statue to Fort Yuma. Then we can get a military escort of cavalry soldiers to help us guard the *Horseman*."

"I do not see that this would help us deliver the statue to your president," Nagata commented, not even looking up from his parchment. "What would be the purpose of this, Mr. Adams?"

"With a little cooperation we could transport the *Golden Horseman* from one army fort to another," Clint explained. "Escorted by armed troops every time we move on to another base. When the military learned it was a gift for the president from the emperor of Japan, I'm sure they'd agree to help us."

"I doubt that," Nagata said, dipping the tip of his brush in an ornate ink well. "Your plan would inform hundreds

59

of soldiers about the *Horseman of Edo,* a golden statue
worth a fortune. The temptation to steal the statue would
be very great. Since American soldiers have no code
similar to Bushido, I doubt that they would be trustwor-
thy. Indeed, I selected my samurai for this mission most
carefully. Our greatest security measure is secrecy, don't
you agree.''

''But the ninja and their outlaw henchmen already
know about the statue,'' Clint reminded him. ''They're
our real enemies. Doesn't it make more sense to concern
ourselves with them instead of worrying about a possible
threat from some greedy soldiers?''

''A threat that will not exist if we do not contact the
American military, Mr. Adams,'' Nagata insisted. ''Besides, your soldiers are not familiar with ninja. They
would be powerless to stop the invisible ones. My samurai
are all experienced with ninja assaults. They are our best
defense against the assassins in black.''

''Don't underestimate American soldiers,'' Clint
urged. ''A lot of them have fought Apaches and other
Indians who are noted for their stealth. I might also add
that cavalrymen might not know what Bushido is, but they
have a code of conduct, and I haven't known many who
don't live up to their own ideals of honor.''

''It is still too risky, Mr. Adams,'' the warlord insisted.
''And I repeat, Americans are no match for ninja. They
are not like your Indians. Ninja might use sword or spear
or poison darts fired from blowguns. They sometimes use
explosives or cannons. They can improvise weapons in
any environment. They are masters of diguise and infil-
tration. They can walk on water or climb the steepest
walls. Ninja can disappear in a puff of smoke and even
hypnotize an opponent with a series of hand motions.''

''But can they cure warts?'' the Gunsmith asked dryly.

"Joke if you like, Mr. Adams," Nagata said sternly. "But ninja are capable of feats which seem impossible. Many believe they have magical powers. You may also believe this before our journey is over."

"If I didn't know better," Clint mused. "I'd think you were looking forward to a confrontation with these ninja agents hired by Heydoor, or whatever that rebel warlord's name is."

"Hedora Fumi," Nagata stated. "His name is Hedora Fumi and I am certain he sent the ninja to steal the *Horseman of Edo*."

"Sounds like you don't like him much," the Gunsmith commented. "Are you sure this isn't just an excuse for a final chance to take him on in combat? Your samurai against his ninja agents?"

"I told you that we're here to deliver the statue to the president," Nagata said, a trace of anger in his voice. "Certainly you don't believe we came to the United States only to fight some sort of feud with Hedora."

"No," Clint assured him. "But it sure seems that you fellas aren't willing to accept a plan of action which would reduce the likelihood of a showdown with Hedora's men. Maybe this is the last opportunity for a samurai battle like in the good old days."

"I'm certain you don't mean to be offensive, Mr. Adams," the warlord said tensely. "But these accusations are insulting, sir. I have already told you why I don't want the cavalry involved. If these explanations do not satisfy you, then I suggest we stop the train, and you may leave now."

"I apologize if I've offended you, Mr. Nagata," Clint told him. "I'll remain with the escort team if you'll promise to reconsider my suggestion. That doesn't mean you have to change your mind about it. I only ask you think about it carefully before you dismiss the idea."

"Agreed, Mr. Adams," Nagata nodded. "Now, is there anything else on your mind?"

In fact the Gunsmith was wondering why Nagata had brought his daughter along for such a dangerous mission, but he decided it wasn't a good time to irritate Nagata anymore. He doubted that there would be a better time in the future.

"No, sir," Clint sighed. "I guess that's all for now."

"Fine," the warlord nodded. "Now, I must get back to writing my journals of this trip, which will later be given to the emperor when I return to Japan."

"Sure," Clint replied. "I'd better get back to my rounds anyway."

ELEVEN

The Gunsmith had decided the best place for him to sleep would probably be at the caboose since it seemed a likely place for invaders to try to jump onboard the platform. Clint also figured the ninja would almost certainly attack at night, so he decided to sleep in the afternoon in order to be wide awake and fully alert by twilight. He learned that Kaiju and two of the other samurai were also following this routine.

Clint entered the caboose and set up his bedroll on the floor. He unbuckled his gunbelt and laid it by the bedroll so it would be within easy reach while he slept. He unbuttoned his shirt and pulled the New Line Colt from its hiding place. The diminutive .22 caliber pistol was an ideal ''belly gun,'' totally concealed when worn under his shirt and tucked into his belt. The small caliber weapon was strictly a close-quarters back-up gun, but it had saved his life on several occasions. The little pistol was quite lethal up to about three yards, but its accuracy and take-down power went to hell beyond that range.

Clint removed his boots and slipped the New Line Colt into one of them. Then he pulled the blinds to the windows of the caboose and sprawled out on the blankets. He tried not to think about any doubts he had concerning the train journey. Clint tried to clear his mind to allow sleep to come. He just hoped he wouldn't dream about creepy men dressed in black and armed with swords.

A door creaked open. Clint sat up, automatically drawing his .45 Colt from leather. A shapely figure dressed in a white kimono stood at the threshold. The woman bowed humbly.

"*Konnichi-wa*, Adam-san," she announced. "I am here to make you happy, yes?"

"Uh . . . that's nice, ma'am," the Gunsmith replied awkwardly. At first he thought the lady was Rikko, but her accent was too thick, and she lacked the other woman's graceful body gestures.

"My name is Hana," she said. "May I enter, Adam-san?"

"If you want," Clint answered, not knowing what else to say under the circumstances.

"Do you want me, Adam-san?" Hana inquired, kneeling beside him on the blankets.

"Want you?" Clint frowned.

"That is what I said," Hana insisted. "Do you want me, Adam-san?"

"Well," Clint answered lamely, "I just met you."

"A man and a woman must know each other if they are to be in love," Hana stated. "But they need meet just a short time to know if they want each other."

Clint smiled. He liked women who were honest and up front about a situation. Hana was certainly attractive, although she lacked Rikko's classic beauty. Hana's face was round, and her nose was a bit larger and flatter than Rikko's, but she was still a very appealing and pretty young lady.

"I want you all right," the Gunsmith decided. "But I'm still wondering why you're here."

"Nagata-sama ask us who want to pillow with Adam-san," Hana explained. "You know pillow?"

"Pillowing," Clint nodded. "I know the expression."

"Everyone of us want pillow with you, yes?" Hana explained, trying to choose her words carefully.

"What do you mean by 'us'?" Clint asked.

"The concubines of Nagata-sama," Hana answered. "He only bring four concubines from Nippon. Three other and me. We had to draw straw to see who win. I am winner, yes?"

"I'll be damned," the Gunsmith muttered.

"No!" Hana exclaimed with alarm. "You not want to be damned. That not good thing to happen to you."

"I didn't mean that literally," Clint replied. He realized she didn't understand him. "It's just an expression of surprise. You understand, Hana?"

"Hai," she smiled and bobbed her head. "Yes, I understand better than all other concubines."

"Your English is a lot better than my Japanese," Clint confessed. "I was just surprised to hear I was first prize, that's all."

"What?" Hana frowned.

"It's not important," Clint assured her. "Uh . . . I don't quite know what to say about pillowing either."

"You want me," Hana answered. "I want you. No need to say more."

She then started to strip off Clint's long-john underwear. The Gunsmith had known a few Oriental women before. Unlike most Western women, Oriental ladies usually undressed the man before taking off their own clothes. Apparently women are used to doing everything for men in the Far East. Clint found this an intriguing cultural trait, although he imagined it could get tiresome if carried to extremes.

After removing the Gunsmith's long johns, Hana stripped off her kimono and got down next to Clint. Her naked body was lovely, with smooth pale skin and tempting curves. Hana's breasts were rather small and her hips a bit wide, but otherwise she was beautiful.

The woman placed her hands on Clint's shoulders and slowly slid her arms around his neck. The Gunsmith kissed her neck, running his tongue along her throat. Clint's hands found her breasts, gently fondling and teasing the nipples until they stiffened under his fingers. The woman moaned with pleasure as Clint moved his hands lower. His lips shifted to her breasts while his fingers traveled to the dark triangle between her thighs.

Hana slowly rose to her knees and slid a leg across Clint's chest. She shifted about and lowered her face to his crotch. Clint slipped his head between her legs and moved his mouth to her womb. The musk scent filled his nostrils as he kissed and licked her vagina. Hana's lips slipped over the head of his penis, drawing the length of his manhood into her mouth.

Clint's tongue slid inside her. He worked it quickly, gradually moving deeper and deeper. Hana's lips rode up and down the Gunsmith's hard member. Clint thrust his tongue faster and harder. Hana gasped in ecstasy as she rapidly approached a climax.

The Gunsmith increased the tempo of his lunges, driving his tongue deeper, burying his face in the center of her womanhood. Hana's mouth moved faster and faster along Clint's throbbing cock. Finally, they both reached the limit. Hana's body convulsed in a magnificent orgasm as the Gunsmith's seed burst inside Hana's skillful mouth.

The couple embraced after making love. The Gunsmith was not a selfish lover.

"I am happy I won," Hana whispered.

"I'm glad too," Clint told her, stroking Hana's hair.

TWELVE

The train moved across the California border into the Arizona Territory. The desert region which comprises much of Arizona is notoriously hot in the summer months, but the weather wasn't unpleasant in early spring, which was the time of season when the train made its journey across the American West.

The Gunsmith was familiar with deserts and knew that the weather can be most unpredictable any time of the year. A heat wave could occur in the middle of winter and the hottest summer day could be followed by a bitter, cold night. It may not rain for months and then, quite suddenly, dark clouds will fill the skies and rain will come pouring down and cause a flash flood.

Clint Adams never cared much for deserts, although the arid wastelands have a strange, primitive beauty unlike any other type of environment. The barren landscape had the purity of simplicity. Rock formations, subjected to centuries of wind and violent rainstorms, were natural sculptures. Many of these were fascinating shapes, stone giants with human features, great archways and staircases etched into boulders by the relentless fingers of time.

The railroad tracks extended between two great rockwalls with numerous boulders lining the ridges of the stony face. Two large boulders blocked the path of the train. The stones sat on the tracks, a solid barricade which had tumbled down from the rockwalls.

But had someone arranged for the boulders to fall?

"I don't like it," the Gunsmith whispered to Kaiju Inoshiro. "If ever a place was ideal for an ambush, this is it."

"I share your concern, Clint," the samurai commander answered. "But the train has already been forced to stop. We'll have to move those boulders before we can continue on our journey."

"Those rockwalls are a perfect hiding place for dry gulchers," Clint stated. "The boulders provide concealment and solid cover. At that elevated position, a couple men with rifles can pick us off before we can move those big rocks off the tracks."

"This may be true," Kaiju admitted. "But we cannot go back, and we cannot stay inside the train. If ninja are involved in such an ambush, they will fire flaming arrows at the train. By setting it ablaze, they will try to smoke us out."

"All right," the Gunsmith began as he worked the lever-action of his Springfield carbine to chamber the first round. "But tell your men to watch the rockwalls. Sure wish some of them knew how to use a rifle."

"Samurai may not be skilled with firearms, Clint," Kaiju replied, gathering up a remarkably long bow and a large quiver of arrows. "But we are trained in *kyujutsu*— combat archery."

Clint glanced down at the bow in Kaiju's fist. It was almost six feet long, longer than Kaiju was tall. The arrows were housed in a box-like wooden quiver over three feet long. The Gunsmith wondered why the Japanese, who tend to be smaller than Americans or Europeans, would use such over-sized weapons.

"The bow is made of a special bamboo called *take*," Kaiju explained. "The wood is lightweight, but very sturdy. The *ebira* quiver holds the traditional twenty-four arrows. These vary in length of shaft and type of arrowhead to serve different purposes. Kyujutsu training takes years, Clint. Before a student is even allowed to touch an arrow, he must perfect the draw of his bow. To do this, he practices by pulling back the bowstring and holding it back for ten minutes at a time. This develops a very steady aim and total muscle control."

"Sounds like fun," the Gunsmith muttered. "But I'll put my faith in a good rifle instead."

"Rifles in Japan are worthless junk," Kaiju snorted. "Old matchlock muskets brought by the Portuguese. The bow is better. Some ninja used rifles and pistols, but they are not as skilled with the bow or the sword."

"Ninja know how to kill people," Clint growled. "That's the only skill they have to have. Don't get arrogant, Kaiju. We can't afford to get careless. Agreed?"

"A wise point, Clint," the samurai nodded. "I assure you, we will not underestimate the enemy."

"All right," the Gunsmith sighed. "Let's go stick our necks out and see what happens."

Clint Adams, Kaiju, and three other samurai climbed down from the passenger cars and stepped off the train. The samurai all carried their kyujutsu gear and swords. The Gunsmith had his Springfield carbine as well as the double-action Colt on his hip and the .22 caliber belly gun under his shirt. Clint glanced about at the rockwalls and the sandy ground at the base of the stony walls. It all seemed void of life. Not even a bird or a lizard stirred as Clint scanned the area.

"You fellers gonna move them boulders?" a voice from the engine shouted. "Luther and me ain't comin' out to help you. Not after what happened at Lawton.''

"Give us a little time, friend,'' Clint replied. "And keep your head down. Both of you.''

"You bet your ass we will!'' a wrinkled old man shouted as he stuck his head out the window of the engine.

A rifle cracked from the rockwall. The old man's skull exploded when a large caliber bullet crashed into it. His corpse tumbled forward and fell to the ground, blood pumping from the jagged stump of his neck.

Clint raised his Springfield, searching for the sniper. He glimpsed the barrel of a rifle as it slipped behind a boulder. Suddenly another gun barrel appeared at another boulder. A stetson-clad head rose up behind the rock. The Gunsmith swiftly altered the aim of his Springfield and squeezed the trigger. The gunman's stetson hopped into the sky as a .45 slug smashed through his head. The sniper's body slumped behind the boulder, and his rifle slipped from his lifeless fingers.

The Gunsmith darted for the engine, using the train for cover from one side of the rockwalls. Another rifle snarled. One of the samurai screamed and fell forward, a bloodied bullet hole between his shoulder blades. Clint jacked a fresh shell in the breech of his Springfield and prepared to aim his weapon at the muzzle flash of the sniper.

Kaiju had already spotted the bastard. The samurai raised his bow and pulled back the string to launch an arrow at the dry gulcher. The missile sailed high and plunged over the top of the boulder. The gunman tumbled into view, the arrow shaft jutting from the side of his neck.

A third sniper opened fire. The bullet ricocheted off the iron frame of the locomotive engine. It hissed past the Gunsmith's face, barely missing the tip of his nose. Clint ducked and peered up at the rocks in time to see the gunman's head before it vanished behind a boulder.

The Gunsmith raised his Springfield and fired three rounds as fast as he could pump the lever and trigger the weapon. Hot shell casings hopped out of the breech. One fell down the back of Clint's collar. The casing burned the Gunsmith's neck, but he ignored the slight discomfort and continued to try to flush out the sniper.

Bullets pelted the rockwall surrounding the boulder which the gunman was using for cover, and ricocheted off stone. The sniper probably felt as if he was being attacked by angry hornets. He rose up and tried to return fire. Clint shot him dead-center in the chest. A samurai unleashed another war arrow aimed at the same target. The missile struck the sniper under the left armpit. He slumped behind the boulder. Nobody was worried that the gunman would get up again.

"That's that," the Gunsmith sighed with relief.

Suddenly, the sand came to life. Half a dozen figures burst up from the ground, hurling loose sand at the faces of the Gunsmith and his samurai allies. The black-suited ninja had hidden under the sand, patiently waiting for their gun-toting henchmen to soften up their opponents.

"Holy shit," Clint gasped as the assassins charged forward, wielding an assortment of exotic weapons.

THIRTEEN

A ninja launched himself at the Gunsmith. The killer carried a weapon which resembled a sickle with a long black handle and a length of iron chain attached to the butt of the shaft. Clint swung his Springfield toward the assailant.

The chain lashed out like a whip. Metal links curled around the barrel of Clint's weapon. The ninja yanked the chain hard and pulled the carbine out of Clint's grasp before he could squeeze the trigger. With a shout of triumph, the ninja raised his sickle and charged.

Clint's hand flashed to the modified Colt on his hip. His incredible reflexes and years of experience and training as a professional gunfighter took over. The Gunsmith cleared leather and fired the double-action pistol in a fragment of a second. The ninja staggered backward when a .45 caliber bullet smashed into his chest. Clint triggered the Colt again and pumped a second round into his opponent. The ninja crashed to earth—dead.

The Gunsmith turned to face another attacker. A long black spear lashed out. The bronze tip of the lance struck Clint's pistol, knocking the barrel off target at the very instant he squeezed the trigger. The Gunsmith's Colt roared, firing a harmless bullet into the ground. The ninja swung the shaft of his spear and slammed the butt across

Clint's wrist. The blow sent the modified Colt revolver flying from his numb fingers.

The ninja slashed the blade of his lance at Clint's face. The Gunsmith jumped back to avoid the attack. His opponent thrust his weapon at Clint's belly. The Gunsmith nimbly sidestepped and seized the lance in both hands. He pulled hard, yanking the startled ninja forward.

Clint quickly dropped backward. His buttocks struck the ground as he raised a boot. The ninja hurtled forward, and Clint's foot caught the man in the midsection. The Gunsmith rolled on his back and pumped his leg hard, kicking the ninja's body. He watched the black-clad figure sail overhead.

However, the ninja didn't crash to the ground in a dazed heap as Clint expected. The assassin released the spear and ducked his head to execute a forward roll. He landed on his feet and instantly drew a sword from his sash.

"Jesus," Clint muttered as he scrambled to his feet, the spear still in his fists.

The Gunsmith was hardly an expert with a lance, but there wasn't time to draw the New Line from inside his shirt. The ninja attacked, slashing his sword at Clint. The Gunsmith raised the spear desperately and managed to slap the shaft against the flat of the ninja's sword. Clint thrust the lance point at the assassin's chest.

The ninja stepped back and slashed his sword at the spear, neatly chopping off the top of the lance. The bronze spearhead dropped to the ground, and the killer in black executed a cross-body sword stroke, aiming his deadly blade at the Gunsmith's neck.

Clint Adams dropped to one knee. The sword slashed overhead. The blade caught his stetson, slicing off the top of the crown without tugging the hat from Clint's head. The Gunsmith quickly rammed the spear shaft forward working it like a cue stick on a billiard table, between the ninja's legs. The killer shrieked as the blow smashed his testicles into pulp.

The Gunsmith jumped to his feet and swung the spear shaft like a club. His first concern was to disarm his opponent so he pounded the stick across the ninja's arms to force him to drop the sword. The assassin reached for the black hilt of a knife in an ankle sheath. Even with his manhood crushed, the ninja was still on his feet and very dangerous.

Clint clubbed him across the skull. The ninja fell to his knees. The Gunsmith hit him again and again until his opponent fell face-first on the ground. Clint kicked him in the side of the head and stomped a boot heel on the back of his neck to be certain the man in black wouldn't get up again.

"Son of a bitch," the Gunsmith rasped breathlessly, turning to see how Kaiju and the other samurai were holding out against the remaining ninja killers.

Kaiju was battling two sword-wielding opponents. The samurai commander had drawn his katana and deftly blocked and parried the ninja swords with his own blade. Kaiju suddenly delivered a karate kick to one ninja's lower abdomen. The man doubled over with a gasp as the samurai turned his attention on the other ninja.

The killer in black raised his sword, but Kaiju took a wide step forward and to the side. The ninja's sword struck only air as Kaiju stepped behind his opponent and slashed his katana across the killer's back. The ninja collapsed to the ground, his spine sliced in two.

The other assassin had recovered from Kaiju's kick to the gut. He suddenly reached inside his black jacket and drew two small star-shaped metal objects from a pocket. The ninja hurled the stars at Kaiju's face. The samurai weaved out of the path of the hurtling weapons as the ninja charged forward.

The killer swung a sword stroke at Kaiju's wrist, hoping to disable and disarm the samurai. Kaiju's katana rose swiftly and deflected the attack. The samurai executed a lightning-fast backhand sweep with his sword and pivoted on one foot to abruptly slash his katana in a downward stroke. The ninja staggered away from Kaiju, blood gushing from a slashed throat and a deep cut in the center of his forehead. The black-clad figure wilted to the ground and died.

Another samurai was pitted against the last ninja attacker. The samurai skillfully warded off his opponent's sword with his katana, but the ninja had more tricks up his sleeve than his ability with a blade. The man in black suddenly jumped back and plucked a small, oval-shaped object from his jacket and hurled it at the samurai. The projectile struck the swordsman's chest and exploded on impact. A bright flash erupted and black powder covered the samurai's face. Blinded, the samurai was unable to stop the ninja from rushing forward and thrusting the point of his sword in the samurai's heart.

Clint Adams located his Colt revolver and scooped it up from the ground. He aimed his pistol at the ninja as the man in black pulled his sword from the slain samurai's chest. The ninja turned just in time to see the muzzle of Clint's gun before the Gunsmith squeezed the trigger. A bullet struck the assassin in the bridge of the nose. It punched through bone and burned into the ninja's brain. Another black-clad corpse fell to the ground.

The Gunsmith and Kaiju glanced about at the lifeless figures which littered the ground. The silence following the battle seemed like a sinister physical force. It was as if the Grim Reaper was claiming the dead—and he might just decide to take Clint and the samurai captain while he was at it.

"The battle is over, Clint," Kaiju said softly. "We have won."

"For now," the Gunsmith replied dryly as he picked up one of the star-shaped weapons which a ninja had thrown at Kaiju.

"Be careful with that, Clint," Kaiju warned. "The metal tines are probably dipped in poison."

"Christ," Clint rasped, dropping the star. "These ninja know every dirty trick in the book—and a few which aren't in print yet."

"Indeed," Kaiju confirmed. "That weapon is called a *shaken,* a throwing star used in the art of *shuriken-jutsu.* Ninja favor such weapons because they can wound or distract an opponent in order to allow the ninja to move in for the kill. Ninja often use instruments which will give them an advantage over their adversary."

"What was that thing one of them threw at the samurai over there?" Clint asked, tilting his head toward the swordsman who had been stabbed to death by the last ninja.

"It is called a *metsubushi* or sight remover," Kaiju explained. "In this case, the weapon was a hollowed out eggshell filled with a simple flash powder and some ground pepper."

"Clever bastards," the Gunsmith muttered. "And they must have had a lot of self-control and discipline to stay buried under that sand for God knows how long."

"No doubt they used hollow reeds or something like that for breathing tubes," the samurai stated, wiping his sword on the jacket of a dead ninja. "It is all part of their training."

"Terrific," the Gunsmith muttered. "I think I could learn to hate ninja without trying too hard."

"Indeed," Kaiju nodded. "When we capture ninja alive, we have them boiled alive or use some other similar type of torture until they are dead. They do not deserve an honorable death. Ninja come from the lower classes, yet they dare to defy the ruling order of the daimyo and samurai classes. Such filth can not be dealt with too harshly."

"Torture?" the Gunsmith frowned.

"We samurai do not do this personally, of course," Kaiju explained. "Torturers are also from peasant stock. No warrior born to the samurai class would lower himself to such a lowly task."

"You'd just have somebody else do your dirty work for you," Clint said dryly. "Tell me, do ninja ever torture samurai when they catch one of you fellas alive?"

"Not that I know of," Kaiju shrugged. "I think they have a code of some sort which forbids them from using torture, similar, perhaps, to the samurai code of Bushido. Of course, they can't hire peasant torturers because they are peasants themselves. Why do you ask, Clint?"

"Just curious," the Gunsmith shrugged. "Let's move the boulders off the track so we can get the hell out of here."

FOURTEEN

The train continued across the Arizona Territory without further incident. The Gunsmith and the Japanese delegation hoped that they had seen the last of the ninja and their American outlaw henchmen. Yet no one was truly convinced that this was true. Lord Nagata and Kaiju Inoshiro had told Clint Adams that it was uncommon for a ninja clan to send more than six ninja agents to handle any task so it was possible that they had already exterminated the entire detachment of black-clad killers sent to retrieve the *Horseman of Edo*.

The Gunsmith wouldn't be able to relax until his mission was finished. After the last encounter with the ninja, Clint wasn't about to dismiss them or underestimate the mysterious men in black. He figured the ninja were as determined to carry out their mission as the samurai were to deliver the gold statue to the president in Washington D.C.

Clint didn't pretend to understand the ninja, but he didn't understand the Japanese who rode with him on the train either. He liked the Japanese. They were very polite and considerate. They bathed every day, which was more than he could say for most Americans he knew. They kept the train cars cleaner than many people keep their own homes.

Yet, Clint also noticed the arrogance of Nagata and his

samurai who considered themselves better than others not born of the higher level of Japanese society. This snobbery included a very calloused attitude toward peasants and a definite racism toward Europeans and Chinese. Clint suspected they also considered themselves culturally, if not intellectually, superior to Americans as well, but they were too polite to make any rude comments to the Gunsmith.

The flaws in the personalities of the Japanese elite were no more unusual than those found among other races. However, the Gunsmith found the Japanese to be basically decent and likeable people. The skills and courage of the samurai and the dedication of Nagata and his followers were certainly admirable.

Clint also found Hana to be an excellent and energetic lover. She was very considerate and eager to please him in bed. They had made love every night since the train journey began. Hana insisted on serving Clint meals and tea, and she waited on him hand and foot although the Gunsmith felt a bit awkward about such attention.

Although he liked Hana and he found her quite satisfactory in bed, he was still strongly attracted to Rikko. The warlord's daughter was not only a rare beauty, but an intelligent and extremely charming lady as well. Rikko possessed the special magnetism which makes a woman truly desirable. He tried to dismiss his feelings, but he couldn't take his eyes off Rikko whenever they met, and he couldn't resist the sexual fantasies about her which inevitably followed.

One of the most difficult things Clint had to deal with aboard the train was Japanese food. The meals consisted of a lot of rice, vegetables, and fish. Most of the food was steamed or boiled, and they regarded *sashimi* as a delicacy. Clint always figured a man only ate raw fish when he only had a can of sardines, or he couldn't light a campfire to fry some trout.

American-bred, the Gunsmith favored meat to fish, but the Japanese diet apparently included very little meat. Clint had some beef jerky among his supplies, but the rations wouldn't last the entire trip. He was glad he had plenty of coffee so he didn't have to drink tea for the journey.

The train came to a halt in New Mexico at a small town called El Mustang. As the name implied, the community was a hybrid of American and Spanish cultures. More than half the buildings were made of adobe with red tile roofs. Passersby wore stetsons or sombreros, and women had shawls draped around their heads. The town appeared to be a quiet, peaceful little place. Clint hoped its appearance wasn't deceptive.

The Gunsmith stepped off the caboose, Springfield carbine canted on a shoulder. Kaiju and another samurai also stepped from the train. Clint saw the engineer climb down from the locomotive.

"Need some help getting coal and wood loaded onboard for fuel?" the Gunsmith inquired as he approached the man.

"I don't need no help with nothin'," the engineer replied sharply. "I'll just collect my money from Naggyta or whatever the head Jap's name is. Then I never wanta see none of you never again!"

"You were hired to drive this train to Washington city," Kaiju told him. "You agreed to do so."

"And I almost got killed twice," the engineer stated. "Poor Luther got his head blown clean off. Had to bury him back there with them heathens and outlaws. Didn't even get a proper headstone. That's the payment Luther got from you jaspers. The same thing ain't gonna happen to me. No sir! I quit right here and now!"

"You knew there could be dangers," Kaiju snapped. "You did not care. You told us you had faced wild Indians before, and the ninja did not frighten you."

"I done changed my mind, feller," the engineer said firmly. "I got you Japs halfway across country, so I reckon you owe me half my pay. I demand it right now!"

"A cowardly peasant demands nothing of a samurai," Kaiju hissed, his fist clenched around the hilt of his katana.

"Hold on, Kaiju," the Gunsmith urged. "If this fella wants to quit, that's up to him. We'll just have to talk to Mr. Nagata and explain to him that our engineer decided to quit, and we'll have to see about getting somebody else."

"If you can find anybody loco enough to take the job," the engineer snorted.

"Fella, you'd better just be quiet and go somewhere out of Kaiju's sight while your head is still on your shoulders," Clint warned. "I'll get your money and bring it to you."

"All right," the engineer agreed with a snivel. "I'll be over at the saloon. Plan to get good and drunk so I won't have to think about everythin' that's happened the last couple days."

"Every man needs a goal in life, friend," Clint said dryly. "Just don't get so drunk you can't count your money when I come looking for you."

"Do you think we can find another man who will know how to run the train, Clint?" Kaiju asked as he watched the engineer head for the saloon.

"I sure hope so," the Gunsmith sighed. "Otherwise we might be sitting on these tracks for a *long* time."

FIFTEEN

"Here's your money, fella," Clint Adams told the engineer as he stepped up to the bar and placed a small leather pouch on the counter. "Two hundred and fifty gold eagles."

"Two fifty?" the man frowned. "I was suppose to get six hundred total. That means I got a full three hundred comin' to me."

"What are you complaining about?" the Gunsmith asked, glancing about the saloon, hoping to see someone dressed in railroad overalls and cap. "New Mexico isn't even a third of the way from California to Washington D.C. You're getting a pretty generous deal, all things considered."

"I reckon it'll have to do," the engineer shrugged. "Goddamn Japs is crazy. You know, I heard a lot about you, Mr. Adams. Never figured you to be exactly crazy before, but if'n you stay with them slant eyes . . . well, folks will kind of wonder about you."

"People have been saying I was crazy for a long time," Clint smiled. "Sometimes I'm inclined to agree with them."

"Yeah," the engineer whispered. "But stayin' with those Japs and sidin' with 'em might make folks wonder if maybe you ain't got no respect for the white race. No

offense, but them slant eyes ain't real popular. Chinks and
Japs just don't fit here in America.''

"But you were still willing to accept Nagata's money,''
the Gunsmith snorted. "I'm getting real tired of listening
to you, fella. I don't like the crap you're talking, and I'm
beginning to really hate your company. Sometimes, when
I feel riled enough, I just draw my gun and smack a fella
across the mouth with the barrel. Bad habit, but reckon I
just can't help myself at times.''

"All right,'' the engineer whined, gathering up a shot
glass and a bottle of red-eye. "I'm movin'.''

The man headed for a table at the opposite side of the
room. Clint turned to the bartender and ordered a beer. He
was glad Kaiju had agreed to wait at the train and let him
try to recruit a new engineer on his own. The samurai's
appearance was more apt to scare away folks or incite
troublemakers than encourage anyone to sign on with the
delegation.

"That'll be five cents,'' the bartender declared, placing
a mug of beer on the counter.

"Here's a dollar,'' Clint replied, placing a single gold
eagle on the counter. "Keep the change.''

"Sounds like you're lookin' for information, mister,''
the bartender remarked, taking the dollar. "Might cost
you a bit more than that.''

"Shouldn't cost too much,'' the Gunsmith told him. "I
just want to know if you can save me a little time. I'm
looking for somebody who has experience as a locomotive
engineer. I need a fella who is available to start work
tomorrow morning. If I can hire on two men, that'll be
even better.''

"There's a number of fellers might be interested,'' the
barman stated. "Of course, I'd have to talk to them
personal like. Time's money, friend.''

"Yeah," the Gunsmith nodded, tossing two more dollars on the bar. "When you talk to them, be sure to mention that the payment will be in gold. They'll be well paid, but the train is heading to Washington D.C. so it's a long haul. Nothing illegal involved. In fact, I'd rather have somebody who wouldn't care if he figured it was illegal. Good chance it'll be dangerous, so be honest when you talk to these fellas. Anybody who shits his breeches in a shoot-out is better off not getting involved."

"Well, now," the bartender scratched his double chin. "I know just the right man for the job. He's a little strange, but he don't mind takin' risks, and he likes money, even if he ain't worth a damn at holdin' onto it."

"You'll talk to him?" Clint said, taking another dollar from his pocket.

"I will," the bartender assured him. "But I can't say for sure he'll accept."

"Two dollars and ninety-five cents seems like enough money for you to just talk to a fella," the Gunsmith commented, holding up the dollar in front of the barman. "I'll give you two more of these if the fella agrees to meet with me, either here in the saloon or out by the train."

"Ain't my fault if he refuses," the bartender shrugs.

"Yeah," Clint nodded as he returned the coin to his pocket. "But now you've got some incentive to talk to this mystery man. You'll also be more apt to be real convincing when you talk to him. Right?"

"Just hope I can be convincing enough," the bartender said with a shrug.

"Tell me his name and tell me where to find him, and you won't have to worry about that," Clint suggested.

"I won't get those other two dollars neither," the barman grinned. "You just have a seat and enjoy your beer, friend. I'll see about gettin' you an engineer."

The Gunsmith turned to walk toward the tables. A beautiful, tall woman with honey-blonde hair and large blue eyes smiled up at him. Clint Adams blinked with surprise when he recognized the woman.

"Hello, Clint," she greeted. "It's been a long time."

"Jenny Parker," the Gunsmith said, a stunned quality in his voice. "My God, what are you doing here?"

"In the town of El Mustang," Jenny smiled, "or in the Siesta Saloon?"

"Both," Clint said. "The last time we met was in Talo, California. You were planning to go to San Francisco to find a job."*

"I wound up here instead," Jenny replied. "And I found a job. Now, I own this saloon. The Siesta is my own private little business. Things have sure changed since we first ran into each other when I was the wife of a farmer in Arizona Territory."†

"You sure don't look any different," Clint remarked. "You still look beautiful, Jenny."

"And you're still one of the most handsome men I ever met, Clint Adams," she stated. "Maybe a little more gray in your hair and an extra wrinkle or two, but on you it looks good."

"Thanks," the Gunsmith said dryly.

"Come on," Jenny began, slipping an arm into the crook of Clint's elbow, "let's chat about old times in private."

---

*Gunsmith #21: Sasquatch Hunt
†Gunsmith #15: Bandit Gold

SIXTEEN

Jenny Parker escorted Clint Adams to a flight of stairs and led him to her bedroom. The Gunsmith had an excellent memory when it came to beautiful women, especially if they were also terrific in bed. Jenny was one of the best—in both categories. Clint remembered her sexual prowess vividly.

"Are you surprised that I've become a business woman?" Jenny inquired as she struck a match to light a kerosene lamp.

"Not really," the Gunsmith replied, closing the door. "Should I lock it?"

"We don't want to be disturbed," she smiled, "do we?"

"I should hope not," Clint replied, turning the key to lock the door.

"You're really not surprised that I didn't get married again and return to the life of a housewife," Jenny remarked, "are you?"

"I don't think being a housewife ever really agreed with you," Clint chuckled. "You're not exactly a one-man woman, Jenny."

"I'm perfectly happy with one man at a time," Jenny grinned.

"But you get a little impatient if you have to wait too long for him," the Gunsmith said dryly. "You're a very intelligent and clever lady. I always figured you had an independent streak about the size of the Grand Canyon, so I'm not surprised you decided to go into business for yourself instead of getting married again.''

"Why thank you, Clint," Jenny smiled as she began to strip off her dark-blue gingham dress. "And here I thought you only admired my body.''

"Well, that too," the Gunsmith confessed. "Maybe I should warn you that I'm just passing through. I'll be on my way tomorrow.''

"You never stay anywhere for long," Jenny commented as she began to remove her undergarments. "Still a traveling gunsmith?''

"Yeah," he answered, unbuttoning his shirt. "But right now I've got a job sort of riding shotgun on a train with a delegation of Japanese.''

"That sounds sort of like the job you'd taken just before we met," Jenny mused. "That one didn't work out so well. Didn't some of the fellas you were with slug you over the head and throw you off the train?''*

"Yeah," the Gunsmith admitted, pulling off his pants. "But I don't think I have to worry about something like that happening this time. Still, there's been a little trouble so far. Hopefully that's over now.''

"Trouble will never be over for you, Clint Adams," Jenny laughed. "You attract it like an old dog attracts fleas. One of these days it's gonna get you killed.''

"Probably," Clint shrugged. "But not tonight.''

Jenny was totally naked now. Her body was still superb. The woman's long swan-like neck gracefully led to her large, round breasts with their pert, pink nipples. Jenny's waist was still lean, her legs long and beautifully shaped. She allowed her eyes to boldly examine the

*Gunsmith #15: Bandit Gold

Gunsmith's nakedness. Obviously, she liked what she saw too.

"Well, Mr. Adams," Jenny smiled. "Shall we lie down for a bit?"

They moved to the bed. Their mouths crushed together. Hands caressed and explored boldly. Their mutual passion boiled over quickly because they already knew how marvelous their lovemaking would be.

Jenny's fingers moved to Clint's rigid penis. Her touch was still magic. Jenny's fingertips rode up and down the fleshy shaft until Clint's cock was throbbing in her hands.

"My, my," Jenny cooed. "I think you're ready."

She straddled the Gunsmith, spreading her legs apart as she mounted him. Clint's hard member found the center of her womanhood. Jenny peeled back the lips of her vagina with one hand and guided his cock with the other. Clint sighed with pleasure as he entered the warm, moist pocket of flesh.

Jenny shifted about, working his penis deeper. Then she began to ride him, breathing hard with sexual labor. Clint resisted the urge to lunge, aware that the time would come. He'd wait until Jenny was ready.

She started to bounce up and down, riding the Gunsmith's fleshy pole with increasing delight. Clint fondled her breasts and arched his back to ram himself home again and again. He followed her rhythm and they continued to paradise together.

Both lovers cried out when they reached the zenith at the same time. Jenny gasped and trembled, digging her fingernails into the carpet of hair on Clint's chest. He groaned breathlessly as his seed burst from his swollen member and jetted inside the woman's cavern of joy.

"Oh, God," Jenny sighed, "that was wonderful. You know, you really are an exceptional man, Clint Adams."

"I think you're pretty special, too," the Gunsmith assured her.

"I'm really glad we got together again," she said, a trace of sadness in her voice. "Even if it is just for tonight, and we'll never see each other again."

"We've sort of got a habit of bumping into each other," Clint commented. "Might be a year or two, but . . ."

"That isn't going to happen again, Clint," Jenny said grimly. "I just know it won't. This will be the last time we'll ever see each other."

"You can't be sure of that," the Gunsmith said.

"I know it, Clint," Jenny insisted. "I just know this'll be the last time."

Somehow, the Gunsmith knew she was right.

"Then let's make the most of tonight," Clint urged.

"You bet," Jenny said with a smile.

SEVENTEEN

"I wondered if you were ever comin' back," the bartender remarked when the Gunsmith strolled into the barroom at three o'clock in the morning.

"I kind of lost track of time," Clint said with a shrug. He glanced about the saloon and noticed only two men seated at a table drinking coffee.

"We closed almost four hours ago, for crissake," the bartender complained. "You're costin' me valuable time, friend."

"Everybody's time is valuable," the Gunsmith stated. "That's why none of us should waste it. Is one of those fellas the train engineer you told me about?"

"That's right," the barman confirmed. "His name is Michael O'Neal. Feller with him is Kelly Malone. They're interested in runnin' your train for you—if the money's right."

"Money is never wrong," Clint remarked. "Sometimes there isn't enough and sometimes you can't accept what folks want you to do to get it, but money itself is never the problem."

"Sure'n it is if you don't have any," one of the men at the table declared. "Come on over here and rest your arse, mate. Let's hear what you've got to say."

The Gunsmith moved to the table and accepted the invitation. He sat across from the pair, wondering which

90

man was O'Neal and whether or not he'd prove to be the right man for the job. One man was wiry and short, with sly dark eyes and a cunning mouth which seemed to turn up at the corners naturally. His companion was a big man, at least six foot four, with a heavy lantern jaw and an impassive face which would have done justice to a samurai.

"I'm Mike O'Neal," the smaller man announced. "This is Kelly. Now, we understand that you need to be takin' that choo-choo train out there to our nation's great capital city, correct?"

"That's right," Clint nodded. "You fellas will get four hundred dollars each."

"Well, now," O'Neal smiled. "You just hired yourself a professional railroad engineer and his trusty train crew, mate."

"Before you accept," Clint began, "I have to warn you that it might be dangerous."

"Oh, shit," O'Neal laughed. "Of course it must be dangerous. You wouldn't offer us four hundred dollars each if it wasn't. We don't mind."

"Let me explain it to you first," the Gunsmith urged.

"Go ahead," O'Neal invited. "But it won't scare off a couple mad Irishmen. For Lord's sake, man, you're talkin' to a couple Irishmen who never drink anything stronger than coffee. Nothin' is crazier than that, mate."

Clint explained the situation. He didn't mention that the *Horseman of Edo* was a golden statue, but he did explain that it was a gift to the president. He told the pair about the ninja and the hired gunmen who had joined forces with the black-clad masters of espionage and death. O'Neal whistled softly.

"Now that's even crazier than Irishmen drinking coffee," he announced.

"Funny little blokes dressed in black outfits who throw metal stars and egg grenades at people?" Malone laughed heartily. "That's the big danger you spoke of?"

"Look," Clint began, "the ninja are dangerous. *Very* dangerous. They are extremely well-trained and the weapons they use aren't toys. I've gone a couple rounds with some ninja, and to be honest, they scare the shit out of me."

"Quite a statement comin' from the Gunsmith," O'Neal commented. "Oh, we know who you are, Mr. Adams. Might figure this whole business was a bloody joke otherwise. If you don't take these ninja lightly, neither will we, but we still want the job. A bit of risk makes life more interesting, eh?"

"All right, fellas," the Gunsmith announced. "You're hired."

The train left El Mustang shortly after dawn. O'Neal and Malone proved to be very professional and handled the job with ease. Clint was relieved and a bit surprised that the Irishmen and the samurai seemed to get along well. The Irish pair were adventurers at heart and not afraid of getting into a scrap or two. This was something the Japanese knight-warriors could certainly understand.

The journey continued smoothly as the train moved on to the Lone Star State. Five days had passed since the last assault on the locomotive, and the delegation began to think that they may have indeed seen the last of the ninja assassins.

Nagata certainly didn't seem to be worried. He tended to drink too much *sake* rice wine and encouraged everyone else to join him. Although the daimyo became less aloof and more pleasant company, Clint worried that his carefree attitude might affect the samurai. Fortunately, Kaiju Inoshiro was the ramrod over the other samurai, and he still shared Clint's concern that the enemy might strike again.

On the evening of the fifth day of tranquility, the train came to an abrupt and unexpected halt. The Gunsmith immediately grabbed his Springfield rifle and headed toward the front of the train. He encountered Kaiju and the remaining samurai in a passenger car. They had gathered up their kyujutsu gear, the box-like quivers of arrows strapped to their backs and longbows held ready in their fists.

"Any idea what happened?" Clint asked the samurai commander.

"Sakata-san was riding in the engine with O'Neal," Kaiju explained. "He was helping the Irishman feed wood and coal to the furnace for fuel. He saw what happened."

"Hai," a short samurai with a stocky physique bowed to the Gunsmith. "Yes, Clint-san. I was with O'Neal-san when he stop train. He had do this because tracks are broken."

"Broken?" Clint frowned. "Christ, somebody must have removed a section of rail."

"But it is so firmly set in the ground," Kaiju remarked. "How could they do this, Clint?"

"With dynamite," the Gunsmith shrugged. "At least that's how I'd do it. I understand derailing a train isn't too hard if you have the right tools and know how to do it. Sure as shit stops the train."

"But how can we repair the tracks so we can continue?" Kaiju asked.

"O'Neal is the expert," Clint replied. "We'll let him

handle that problem. We'd better be concerned with whatever kind of trap the ninja and their pals have in store for us.''

"We are ready for them," Sakata announced, holding his bow high.

"One is never ready for ninja," Kaiju said sharply. "They strike like deadly mist, silent and all but invisible. You should not brag, Sakata-san. It is unseemly for a samurai."

"*Wakari-masu, Kaiju-san*," Sakata said, humbly lowering his head. "I apologize for my behavior."

"Let's go see what kind of surprises the boys in black have for us this time," the Gunsmith suggested.

EIGHTEEN

The Gunsmith peered out a window. The train had come into a woodland area. Trees surrounded the railroad tracks. Plenty of cover for snipers or ninja assassins. Clint didn't care to step outside and present a clear target for the enemy.

"Wait a minute," the Gunsmith told his samurai companions. "Does anybody have a spare robe I can use?"

"A kimono, Clint?" Kaiju inquired, raising an eyebrow with surprise.

"I'd use mine but it's a personal gift from your warlord," Clint explained. "Besides, I left it back at the caboose. I also need two pieces of wood. One should be about a yard long. The other should be as long as possible. One of those spears you samurai keep on the weapon racks would be perfect."

"You mean a *naginata*?" Kaiju asked.

"I mean a spear or whatever you call those big hooked blades at the end of those long poles," Clint replied, a bit more curtly than he intended. The Gunsmith didn't feel like getting a lesson on Japanese terms when they were surrounded by killers.

Kaiju barked a curt order in Japanese. One of the samurai quickly fetched the weapon and a bamboo stick roughly a yard long. Clint placed the smaller stick across the shaft of the naginata, just below the blade, and tied it down with a length of rope.

"I think I understand now," Kaiju commented as he handed Clint a kimono. "We are making a dummy, yes?"

"You guessed it," Clint confirmed, checking his handiwork. The crossed sticks formed a crude T frame. "Give me a hand with the robe, Kaiju."

They slipped the kimono over the top of the frame, using the bamboo cross section to fill out the sleeves. The Gunsmith held the shaft at the end and extended the improvised "dummy" figure toward a door.

"All right," Clint began. "Somebody open the door. I'll stick this scarecrow outside, and we'll see what happens. Everybody else keep your arrows ready on the bows and watch for muzzle flashes and evidence of enemy ninja. Be careful when you look out the windows. Don't give the enemy another target. We want them to concentrate on the dummy."

Kaiju quickly translated the instructions to the samurai who did not understand English. They nodded in agreement and drew arrows from their quivers. The samurai archers moved to windows and waited.

"All right," Clint announced. "Open the door and stand clear."

Kaiju obeyed the Gunsmith's instructions. He opened the door, and Clint slowly extended the scarecrow figure at the end of the naginata. He poked the kimono-clad dummy outside. The tactic produced results immediately. A rifle shot erupted from the forest and a lead projectile ripped a hole in the kimono. Another shot cracked and a second bullet punctured cloth.

Two samurai archers unleashed arrows, firing the missiles right through the glass panes of windows. The arrows shattered small sections of glass and hurled out into the forest. The archers had aimed at the muzzle flashes of the snipers' weapons. A shriek from somewhere among the trees signaled a hit.

Suddenly two objects struck the kimono dummy. Flames danced from two star-shaped shaken which had been soaked in kerosine and set afire before they were thrown. The kimono and the wooden frame began to burn. Clint hurled the flaming remnants outside.

"Damn ninja tricks," the Gunsmith rasped as he grabbed his Springfield carbine.

Something struck a window and an explosion shattered glass. A samurai screamed and fell backward, both hands clamped over his eyes. Probably another eggshell filled with flash powder and pepper, Clint thought. The ninja were using similar tactics as before. They realized the hired gunmen, armed with rifles, were more effective from a distance. Thus they used the gunmen to cover their own attack as they closed in to fight their style—close-quarters and sneaky as hell.

Clint fired his Springfield, pumping a hasty round through the open door. He didn't intend to hit any of the unseen assassins, but he hoped to encourage them to back off for a moment or two. A rifle snarled from the darkness beyond and a bullet splintered wood from the door frame. Clint jacketed a fresh round into the breech of his carbine and fired at the enemy muzzle flash. A scream rewarded his efforts.

The Gunsmith swiftly moved away from the doorway. Two shaken stars whirled across the threshold, narrowly missing Clint. Kaiju suddenly drew a small, thin bladed knife from the scabbard of the short sword in his sash. The samurai's arm flashed as he threw the blade at a shadow which lurked by some bushes near the tracks. The ninja screamed and fell to his knees with Kaiju's knife buried in his chest.

"You fellas know some dirty tricks, too," Clint remarked.

"The *kozuka* throwing knife is an honorable samurai weapon," Kaiju replied. "Not a dirty trick."

"Whatever you say," Clint agreed as he listened to gunshots which echoed from the front of the train. "Sounds like O'Neal and Malone are trading lead with some of the bastards."

"We can't help them right now," Kaiju remarked. "We have enemies to worry about right here."

"Is anybody at the rear of the train?" the Gunsmith asked. "That is, besides Hana?"

"I do not believe so," the samurai frowned. "I'll send one of the men to check on her."

"No," Clint replied, "I'll do it. You take care of things here."

"Very well," Kaiju nodded grimly. "Be careful, my friend."

"You, too," the Gunsmith urged.

Clint headed for the rear of the train. He opened the door cautiously and peered outside. The Gunsmith saw no one lurking in the shadows, but that didn't necessarily mean no one was there when one is dealing with ninja. He slowly eased the door open wider.

Then Clint glanced down and noticed a thread attached to the door. The cord was pulled taunt, and Clint heard something click in the shadows. He threw himself backward and dropped to the floor, instinctively covering his head.

A short arrow-like projectile was fired from a crossbow booby-trap. The bolt hissed through the doorway and sizzled over the Gunsmith's prone form. Clint heard the missile slam into a wall somewhere behind him. He uncovered his head and gazed up at the doorway to see a black figure appear at the threshold.

The Gunsmith swung his Springfield toward the invader and squeezed the trigger. The carbine roared and a .45 caliber projectile kicked the ninja backward to tumble over the handrail to the platform. The assassin seemed to vanish in the blink of an eye.

Clint started to rise when another ninja entered. The killer in black hissed like a snake as he slashed a sword at the Gunsmith's head. Clint didn't have time to work the lever action of his carbine. He raised the Springfield and held it up like a bar to block the attacking blade.

Clint turned sharply and delivered a butt-stroke, slamming the walnut stock of his carbine across the ninja's arms. The blow struck the sword from his opponent's grasp, but the ninja swiftly snap-kicked Clint in the gut. The Gunsmith groaned and doubled over from the blow as the killer slipped behind him.

The ninja grabbed the barrel and stock of Clint's Springfield and pulled it across the Gunsmith's throat. The bastard was trying to throttle Clint with his own gun. Clint grabbed the frame of the carbine and tried to pull it away from his throat, but the ninja was strong and trained in the use of leverage.

Clint kicked both feet into a wall and sent himself hurtling backward, taking the ninja assassin with him. Both men plunged through the open doorway and staggered onto the platform. They collided against the handrail. The ninja groaned when his spine connected with iron. Clint quickly rammed an elbow into the killer's ribs, then he pulled the Springfield again.

This time he yanked the barrel from under his chin. The

Gunsmith used his greater size and strength to raise the carbine overhead, although the ninja still held onto it. Then Clint dropped to one knee and bent forward to send his opponent hurtling overhead in an abrupt flying mare. The ninja sailed over the platform and crashed to the ground below.

The Gunsmith didn't know if he'd killed the assassin or simply knocked him unconscious. At the moment, he didn't care. Clint hurried across the coupling to the next passenger car, pumping the lever of his Springfield as he ran.

Clint yanked open the door. A long black spear lunged for his belly. The Gunsmith parried the attack with the barrel of his carbine and deflected the spear shaft. The bronze point stabbed into the door frame near Clint's hip. He quickly slashed a backhand sweep with the Springfield and whipped the barrel of his weapon across the attacking ninja's face.

The blow sent the black-suited killer reeling. The assassin hit the floor, rolled, and landed on one knee. He reached for the haft of a sword in his sash. The Gunsmith braced the Springfield against a hip, snap-aimed and triggered the weapon. The ninja's face exploded when 230 grains of lead smashed into it.

"Jesus," the Gunsmith rasped breathlessly. "These sons of bitches are coming outta the goddamn woodwork!"

He jogged through the passenger car to the opposite end and carefully opened the door. There were no booby-traps this time. He even managed to cross over to the next car without being harassed. As he prepared to open the door to the caboose, a figure appeared from the shadows.

It wasn't a ninja this time. The man wore a battered old stetson, and he carried a Winchester tucked under his arm.

The outlaw hadn't noticed Clint. He was creeping along the side of the train, his attention centered on the cars up ahead.

"Hey, fella?" the Gunsmith whispered.

The man turned sharply and stared up at the Gunsmith. Clint kicked him in the face, driving the heel of his boot into the point of the gunman's jaw. The outlaw fell unconscious. Clint made a mental note to look for the bastard later.

He entered the caboose, Springfield carbine held ready. Two figures lay on the bedroll, blankets stained with blood. One was a dead ninja, the hilt of a knife jutting from his heart. The other was the body of Hana. Her throat had been slashed open. The ninja's sword was still in his fist. The blade was stained with blood.

"Oh, Hana," the Gunsmith shook his head sadly. "I should have been here, damn it!"

NINETEEN

The battle ended as suddenly as it had begun. The shooting stopped and a thorough search assured them that there were no living ninja in any of the train cars. The Gunsmith had covered Hana's body and returned to the main passenger car where he met with Kaiju Inoshiro, the warlord Nagata, and his lovely daughter Rikko. Clint told Nagata his concubine was dead.

"She apparently fought with one of the ninja," Clint explained. "They killed each other."

"An honorable death," Nagata said, nodding his head.

"Hai, Nagata-sama," Kaiju agreed. "Hana will surely be granted a better life in her next incarnation."

"Maybe she'll be lucky enough to be born a man next time," Rikko muttered softly. Clint was the only one who heard her remark.

"I'm touched by how upset you folks are," the Gunsmith said dryly, but he immediately regretted the statement. "Sorry. I've got no right to judge how you choose to grieve Hana's death."

"We can only grieve the loss we suffer," Nagata explained. "Hana's fate will not be unfortunate."

"Then maybe she'll be better off than us," the Gunsmith said. "Because the enemy broke off the attack doesn't mean they aren't still out there trying to figure out how to hit us next."

"Hullo, chaps," Michael O'Neal said cheerfully as he entered the car. "Looks like we held up a lot better than those bloody morons what jumped us."

"One samurai and a lady passenger were killed," Clint told him. "Another samurai was blinded. I wouldn't say that's reason to celebrate, fella."

"The samurai who was blinded by the metsubushi?" Kaiju inquired. "He has recovered, Clint. The flash and pepper did not cause permanent damage to his eyes."

"Glad to hear it," the Gunsmith assured him. "Guess his karma was favorable, huh?"

"Indeed," Kaiju nodded, failing to notice Clint's sarcasm. "I'm glad you understand."

"Well, I don't mean to make light of the deaths that occurred back here," O'Neal said. "But it appears we won the first round at least. Kelly and me shot three blokes, including one of those buggers dressed in black. Pardon my language, ma'am."

"That's quite all right," Rikko assured him.

"By the way," O'Neal added. "You were right about those fellows in black being sneakier than British perverts."

"I don't recall making that comparison," the Gunsmith said dryly.

"Maybe not," the Irishman shrugged. "Anyway, one of those sneaky blokes actually managed to creep inside the engine. Kelly and me didn't even see him until he drew a sword. Kelly hit him with a blast of buckshot just in time. We 'bout peed our drawers. Sorry again, ma'am."

"What about the track?" Clint asked. "Can we get out of here?"

"Not until we've put down some rails to replace the section which ain't there no more, mate," O'Neal explained.

"Is that possible?" Nagata inquired.

"It wouldn't be if Kelly and me hadn't brought along some tools and about half a ton of iron rail," the Irishman grinned. "Told you we're professionals. Try to plan for every emergency, I say. Take us about four or five hours—that's providing we get help from you chaps."

"Great," the Gunsmith snorted. "We're supposed to go out in the open for five hours and nail down rails while we're still surrounded by ninja and outlaws? That'll give them enough time to chop down trees and drop 'em on our heads."

"I know it's not the most desirable notion," O'Neal admitted. "But we haven't much of a choice, have we? I suppose we could stay inside the train and wait until dawn if you think that would be safer, but we'll still have to repair that track before this train is going anywhere."

"Before we decide," the Gunsmith began, "I think we ought to have a talk with somebody I left outside. Fella is probably still taking a nap, but he's still alive."

"If he is a ninja, don't expect him to tell us anything," Kaiju warned. "Ninja have been known to bite off their own tongues to remain silent. Some have even slashed their faces to avoid revealing their identity in case this could lead to discovering the rest of their clan."

"Fella's an American-bred outlaw," Clint assured the samurai. "And I suspect we can get him to talk, but we'd better get the son of a bitch before he wakes up and crawls off to the trees."

"Or the ninja kill him to insure his silence," Kaiju added.

Clint and Kaiju found the man the Gunsmith had kicked in the face. The outlaw had just begun to recover consciousness when Clint and Kaiju pulled him to his feet and hauled the man inside the passenger car. The Gunsmith covered Kaiju, holding his Springfield carbine ready.

They escorted the dazed outlaw into the main passenger car and dumped him on the floor. The man stared up at his captors. His vision gradually cleared, and he recognized one of them.

"Jesus Christ!" the hoot owl gasped. "You're Clint Adams!"

"That's right," the Gunsmith nodded. "What's your name, fella?"

"What the hell is the Gunsmith doin' ridin' on a train full of Japs?" the man asked.

Kaiju kicked him in the ribs. The man yelped in pain.

"You were asked a question, scum!" the samurai snapped. "Tell us your name. Now!"

"Look, fella," Clint sighed. "You're already wearing my bootprint on your face. If you don't want to answer us, we'll just kick you all around the room until you feel like talking. We don't want to have to do that because you might have trouble answering us while you're pissing blood."

"My name's Hal Culpepper," the outlaw said quickly.

"That's better," Clint said. "Who do you work for, Hal?"

"I'm a member of Jake Burrows' Gang," Culpepper announced. "Ever heard of them, Adams?"

"Sure," the Gunsmith grinned. "Burrows probably has the largest gang of incompetent outlaws in the West."

"What does incompetent mean?" Jake frowned, unsure whether or not the term was an insult.

"It means you and the other members of Burrows' Gang are a bunch of idiots," Clint explained. "It means you fellers are too dumb to unbutton your trousers when you have to take a piss."

''You ain't got no call for bad-mouthin' me that way,
Adams,'' Culpepper pouted. ''And the Burrows Gang
ain't nobody you'd wanta mess with.''

''The only threat the Burrows gang has ever been was
that reading about how you morons screwed up is enough
to make a fella bust a rib laughing,'' the Gunsmith stated.
''The Burrows Gang was the bunch that tried to rob that
army payroll train a few years ago? The one near Fort
Yuma? Thirty of you halfwits attacked the train. It was
full of soldiers, naturally, so half of you got shot out of the
saddle before dumb ol' Jake had enough sense to retreat.''

''Reckon we didn't plan that job too good,'' Culpepper
admitted lamely. ''But we learned better after that.''

''Sure,'' Clint laughed. ''That's why you fellas did so
well in Laredo. About a dozen of you rode into town, all
dressed in cattlemen slickers, dark stetsons and necker-
chiefs tied under your chins. You may as well have worn
masks to let everybody know you were planning to rob the
bank.''

''We looked like cattlemen, damn it,'' Culpepper insisted. ''Goddamn sheriff just made a lucky guess.''

''That's why the sheriff rounded up a town militia as
soon as he saw you idiots head for the bank,'' Clint
commented. ''Way I heard it, the bank tellers already had
guns drawn before you boys even entered the place. You
jackasses got caught in a crossfire. It was a miracle any of
you managed to get out of Laredo alive.''

''Just had some bad luck is all,'' Culpepper sniveled.
''Looks like I'm in for some more bad luck now,too.''

''You're a little fish,'' Clint told him. ''We're concerned about the big ones. Now, how many of you fellas
are left?''

''Only 'bout five or six now,'' the outlaw answered.
''Some of the gang got scared and ran out on us. Couple

others tried, but the Japs killed 'em. Mean fellers, them Japs.''

"You refer to the ninja?" Kaiju asked. "The men dressed in black?"

"The other Japs called 'em 'shadow warriors,' " Culpepper stated. "The head Jap told us they'd be workin' with us, and we was supposed to follow orders from the feller in charge of the shadows. Clever little bastard, but it wasn't the shadow men what killed our boys. Was a Jap dressed up like you. Carryin' two swords and wearin' his hair that funny way. Like he figured he was part Mohawk Indian or somethin'.''

"A samurai?" Clint frowned. "Is that possible, Kaiju?"

"A samurai in the United States of America?" Kaiju smiled. "Don't be absurd, Clint."

"I mean a samurai working with ninja," the Gunsmith explained. "You fellas don't seem to get along due to the difference in class levels and all."

"Ninja are hired by daimyo warlords," Kaiju replied with a shrug. "And we samurai are bound by the code of Bushido to obey our daimyo masters' wishes. If a warlord orders a samurai to work with ninja, then the samurai would have to obey."

"So the daimyo back in Japan who sent the ninja also sent a samurai to sort of ramrod the mission," Clint remarked. "Guess he didn't trust the ninja to steal the *Horseman of Edo* and return it to Japan."

"No, Hedora would not trust anyone except his most trusted samurai with anything so valuable." Kaiju turned to Culpepper. "The samurai in charge of the others, he spoke English, yes?"

"Yeah," the outlaw nodded. "And he had a black patch over his left eye. You know him?"

"Hai," Kaiju confirmed. "I know who he is. The description makes this certain. The samurai in charge is Yamato Fujo. He is Hedora's samurai commander and a daimyo himself, although his rank is lower than Hedora's of course. Yamato is very respected and feared in Japan. He is quite brilliant and a master swordsman, regarded as one of the best in all Nippon."

"He can't be too smart, or he wouldn't have hired Jake Burrows and his gang of brainless wonders," Clint muttered.

"Maybe he didn't know about our reputation," Culpepper sighed, no longer trying to defend the good name of his gang.

"Maybe," the Gunsmith mused. "Or, maybe he figured you boys would be perfect cannon fodder."

"You mean he wants to get us killed?" Culpepper glared at Clint. "What would he want to do that for?"

"Nothing personal," Clint assured him. "It's just that Yamato wants the *Horseman of Edo*, and he's willing to do whatever he has to in order to get it. He's also trying to steal something which actually belongs to the emperor of Japan until it's delivered to the president. Don't reckon he'd want any witnesses to tie him in with something like that."

"Jesus, Mary, and Joseph," Culpepper rasped. "Maybe I'm lucky you fellers caught me after all."

"Not too lucky, Hal," the Gunsmith told him. "Yamato wants us dead, too."

TWENTY

At dawn, Michael O'Neal supervised the repair of the rails. Clint Adams, Kaiju Inoshiro, and Sakata, the best samurai archer, stood guard while several others worked on the tracks. A reluctant Hal Culpepper helped to set the new sections of rail. The outlaw didn't have much choice. He could either do as he was told or take his chances with the enemy which lurked somewhere in the forest.

Or did they?

The night had passed slowly. Everyone had endured the tension of waiting for the enemy to strike again, but nothing happened. They were equally fearful of an attack while they worked on the railroad that morning. However, the men completed the task without incident.

"Looks like we've been sweatin' bullets for nothin'," O'Neal commented, wiping his sweaty brow. "The bastards really retreated."

"Maybe we killed them all," Kelly Malone suggested, canting a sledgehammer over his shoulder. "Could be this whole mess is over now."

"Don't bet on it," Clint warned. "The fellas we're dealing with aren't the type to give up."

"Neither are we," Kaiju declared.

"That's a fact," the Gunsmith agreed.

O'Neal and Malone climbed into the engine and the

109

others boarded the passenger cars. A few minutes later the train was rolling on the tracks. It increased speed and soon roared across the iron rails.

The Gunsmith decided to check on Duke to see how the big black gelding was handling the trip. Clint entered the cattle car. He was surprised to discover Rikko, tenderly brushing the white coat of a small mare in one of the stalls.

"Hello, Clint," Rikko greeted. "I see you were concerned about your horse, too. He's quite a magnificent animal."

"Yes, he is," the Gunsmith agreed. "That's a mighty pretty mare you've got, too. What's her name?"

"Her name is Yoake," Rikko replied. "It means dawn—the beginning of a new day. I have always thought of dawn as a symbol of hope. Do you understand?"

"I think so," Clint smiled. "I haven't had much chance to get to talk to you, but I've always been pleased when I've had the opportunity."

"I have been pleased to talk to you also, Clint," Rikko said. "You're not at all like I expected Americans to be. In Japan, we were taught to believe Americans are all uncultured barbarians."

"Well, some Americans are," the Gunsmith shrugged. "But a few of us are cultured barbarians."

She laughed. "Please do not be offended. In Japan, we consider everyone else to be barbarians. It's an old tradition of the ruling class. I understand European monarchs have a similar attitude. Is it true you Americans fought a war in order to do away with rule by the elite of Britain."

"Something like that," Clint answered. "We elect fellas to represent us in government instead. Some of them don't do such a good job so we vote them out and put other fellas in power instead."

"I can't imagine such a system working," Rikko

frowned. "It seems that it would be very confusing getting a new government all the time. I'm surprised you don't have armed revolutions by those who are unhappy with the current government. After all, anyone in the United States can own a gun."

"We don't exactly get a different government," Clint explained. "See, the Constitution lays down certain rules so the fellas in office can't overstep their bounds."

"A very strange system," Rikko sighed.

"It's worked out so far," Clint told her. "And we've been using it for more than a hundred years now."

"A hundred years is not very long," Rikko stated. "The history of Japan covers many centuries."

"Everybody has to start somewhere," the Gunsmith shrugged. "What is it like being the daughter of a warlord?"

"I am better off than most women in Japan," Rikko answered. "But I am not equal to any man in my class. But this is true everywhere, yes? American women are not equal to American men, correct?"

"Not yet," Clint admitted. "But that might change if a lot of women get their way."

"Did you love Hana?" Rikko asked, after a moment of silence.

"Uh, well," the Gunsmith began awkwardly, caught off guard by Rikko's question. "No, I didn't love Hana, but I liked her. Your father probably knew her better than I did."

"I doubt that," Rikko said. "Concubines are cattle. Their owners don't try to understand them. A concubine simply follows orders. The subject of personalities seldom comes up in such a relationship."

"What does your mother think of these concubines?" Clint asked dryly. "Never mind, I shouldn't have asked."

"My mother accepts the situation as karma," Rikko smiled. "Fate rules all our lives, whether we like it or not."

"Maybe," Clint replied. "And maybe that's just an easy way to excuse our mistakes."

"I see," Rikko nodded. "You blame yourself for Hana's death, yes?"

"I shouldn't have left her in the caboose alone," the Gunsmith said.

"You could not be everywhere at once, Clint," Rikko told him. "You tried to reach her and help protect her from the ninja, but her karma was death."

"Thanks," the Gunsmith said. "I appreciate what you're trying to do, but I'm gonna feel bad about Hana for a while. Not enough to interfere with my job, but I'll still be a little upset."

"That is understandable," the woman agreed. "But remember guilt is a useless emotion which can only take away your energy and produce nothing."

"How did somebody as young and beautiful as you get to be so wise?" Clint grinned.

"Perhaps that is my karma," Rikko replied with a smile.

Clint glanced over her shoulder and saw a door silently open. A figure in black slipped through the gap. The shadow held a bow in one fist and pulled back an arrow notched to the string. The Gunsmith immediately shoved Rikko aside, pushing her into an empty stall. His hand streaked for the Colt on his hip as the ninja released his arrow.

The revolver cleared leather and roared, flame spitting from the muzzle. Lead smashed into wood and splinters exploded in midair. The ninja uttered an expression of astonishment.

The Gunsmith had literally shot the arrow in flight.

The ninja realized he couldn't draw and fire another arrow fast enough to beat the Gunsmith's trigger finger. The killer's right hand moved to his left wrist and suddenly drew a six-inch iron spike from a forearm sheath. He raised his arm to hurl the throwing spike. Clint Adams shot him twice through the heart. The ninja fell back against the nearest stall and slumped lifeless to the floor.

An oval-shaped object hurled through the open doorway. The Gunsmith turned away from it and covered his face with his arms before the projectile struck the floor. The eggshell shattered, detonating flash powder and spewing pepper across the cattle car. Horses neighed angrily as the debris assaulted their nostrils.

Clint uncovered his eyes and turned to face the second ninja who charged across the threshold, an old bronze pistol in his fist. The ninja triggered his ancient matchlock gun. Flames burst from the hammer and pan, and the barrel roared. A large caliber lead ball crashed into the post of a stall less than a foot from the Gunsmith. Splinters burst from the wooden pillar. Several sharp shards pierced Clint's sleeve and bit into his arm.

The Gunsmith clenched his teeth and mentally shut out the sting in his upper arm as he aimed the modified double-action Colt revolver at the ninja. He fired the six-gun. The man in black had discarded his bronze single-shot pistol and reached for the hilt of his sword. A 230 grain lead projectile struck the ninja's right forearm.

The bullet split bone. The ninja cried out in pain as the impact of the bullet spun him about like a top. Most men would have fallen to the floor, overpowered by agony, but the ninja suddenly charged forward and shouted a battle cry as he leaped into the air.

Clint hastily fired his pistol again. The bullet burned the

air beneath the hurtling form of the ninja. Clint tried to adjust the aim of his weapon, but he didn't have time. The ninja rocketed into him, driving a foot into the Gunsmith's chest.

The kick knocked the Gunsmith flat on his back. The Colt revolver was jarred from his hand when he hit the floor. Clint stared up at the ninja. The killer's right arm dangled uselessly, blood dripping from the shattered limb. The ninja staggered slightly and fell to his knees beside Clint. The assassin's left hand yanked a small dagger from a sheath under his jacket.

TWENTY-ONE

Clint Adams lashed out a boot and kicked the ninja in the face before the killer could use his blade. The man in black grunted and crashed to the floor. Clint scrambled forward and pounced on his opponent, grabbing the wrist behind the assassin's knife.

The Gunsmith twisted the man's wrist, trying to force him to drop the knife. The ninja bent a knee and whipped it into Clint's left kidney. The Gunsmith groaned, but held onto the killer's wrist. The ninja hooked the front of his right elbow into the side of Clint's jaw. The blow toppled Clint. Suddenly the ninja was on top, the dagger still in his fist.

Then a loop of metal links flashed over the ninja's head and a chain encircled his neck. Rikko pulled the weighted ends of the chain as she planted a foot between the ninja's shoulder blades. The woman yanked hard. The killer in black uttered an ugly gurgling sound as he desperately tried to pry the chain with the blade of his knife.

Rikko pulled harder. The ninja awkwardly tried to slash his weapon backward at Rikko. He missed. The killer's eyes bulged, and his tongue hung from his gaping mouth as his face adopted a red-and-purple hue. The ninja tried another feeble knife slash. His blade scraped the floor as his eyes rolled up in his head.

Clint was too stunned to do anything but watch. Rikko

continued to throttle the ninja until she was certain the last flicker of life had been snuffed out. Then she unwound the weighted chain from his neck and let the ninja's corpse slump to the floor.

"Lady," the Gunsmith said softly, "you're sure full of surprises."

"Violence is sometimes necessary," Rikko stated. "Even for a woman. Are you all right, Clint?"

"I'm still alive," the Gunsmith replied, rubbing his sore jaw. "Thanks to you."

"You saved my life from the ninja archer," she declared. "Neither of us need feel a debt to the other."

"That's nice," Clint said as he retrieved his double-action Colt. "But we'd better tell the rest that the train is under attack again. Sneaky ninja bastards must have climbed on during the first battle when we had to stop because of the missing rails. They've probably been riding on the roofs of the cars or even clinging to the framework underneath."

"With ninja anything is possible," Rikko stated.

"That's a fact," the Gunsmith agreed.

The couple moved to the door at the end of the car. Clint opened it carefully, his .45 pistol held ready. The Gunsmith peered outside, leery of ninja tricks. He saw nothing. Clint nodded to Rikko, and they stepped onto the platform.

Clint and Rikko crossed over the coupling to the next car. The Gunsmith leaned against the door to the passenger compartment. He heard steel clash against steel, and the furious war shouts of samurai and ninja combatants.

"Sounds like Kaiju and the others already know we're under attack," Clint whispered as he prepared to open the door.

Suddenly, a sword blade slashed air inches from the tip of Clint's nose. He recoiled from the flashing steel and bumped into the handrail. The head and right shoulder of a ninja leaned over the edge of the car roof, a sword clenched in his fist.

Rikko's weighted chain lashed out like the tongue of a serpent. Metal links whirled around the blade of the assassin's sword. She yanked the chain hard, pulling the sword away from the Gunsmith. Clint stepped forward and jammed the muzzle of his Colt under the ninja's jaw. He squeezed the trigger. A .45 bullet punched through the roof of the ninja's mouth, tunneled through his brain, and blew off the top of his skull.

"Shit," Clint rasped as he watched the black-clad corpse tumble from the roof to be crushed to pulp by the great iron wheels of the train.

The Gunsmith suddenly realized he had forgotten to reload his pistol, and he only had one bullet left. There wasn't time to do it at the moment so he reached inside his shirt and drew the New Line with his left hand.

"You have some surprises, too," Rikko mused as she held her fighting chain, hands fisted around the weighted ends.

"Sometimes it helps a fella stay alive," the Gunsmith replied. "Stay back. Don't get into the fight unless you have to."

The Gunsmith opened the door. Inside the passenger car, three samurai were locked in combat with four ninja. Two black-clad killers were trading sword strokes with Kaiju Inoshiro. The samurai commander seemed to be holding off his opponents pretty well, but the other samurai were in trouble.

Sakata was the best archer among the samurai, but he wasn't as formidable with a sword as he was with a bow.

His ninja opponent was armed with a long-handled sickle weapon equipped with a long chain at the end. The assassin whipped the chain around Sakata's sword, snaring the blade. He pulled the chain hard, yanking the samurai's sword to the side as he closed in and raised the sickle weapon to finish off Sakata.

Clint aimed his .45 Colt and fired. A bullet crashed into the side of the ninja's head, bursting his skull like a watermelon struck by a sledgehammer. Sakata turned to the Gunsmith and bowed. Clint barely nodded in reply as he hastily holstered his empty Colt and swapped the .22 New Line from his left hand to his right.

Kaiju used the flat of his katana to block a sword stroke and abruptly shifted his weight to shove the blades toward the other ninja opponent. The second killer's sword rang against his comrade's weapon. Kaiju had adroitly slipped his katana from his first opponent's blade. The ninja stared at each other, startled to find themselves crossing swords with each other instead of the samurai. Kaiju delivered a panther-quick sideways sweep with his weapon. The blade of his katana slashed under both ninja's chins. The assassins stumbled backward, blood flowing from their sliced throats. They wilted to the floor and died.

The third samurai was pitted against a lone ninja who wore a set of iron claws strapped to both hands. The swordsman attempted an overhead cut with his katana. The ninja's arms rose and his hands clapped together, trapping the blade of his opponent's sword between the iron talons.

The ninja's right foot delivered a quick snap-kick and raked another set of iron claws across the samurai's lower abdomen. The warrior screamed as blood poured from the terrible wound. A purplish intestine poked from the tear like a giant worm. The ninja chopped the side of a hand across the samurai's wrist and struck the sword from his grasp.

The killer's other hand slammed an open palm blow to the samurai's face. The swordsman bellowed in agony as metal claws ripped flesh and punctured his right eyeball. The ninja then seized the warrior's throat and yanked hard, tearing it open with his deadly iron talons. The samurai fell, probably grateful to be dying.

"Son of a bitch," Clint rasped as he aimed the New Line Colt at the ninja.

"No, Clint," Kaiju urged as he stepped toward the last killer in black. "Please, he is mine."

"Watch yourself, friend," the Gunsmith replied, lowering his pistol.

The ninja turned to face Kaiju, blood dripping from the iron claws strapped to his hands. Kaiju held his katana high, fists clenched around the sword hilt above his head. He shuffled closer and shouted as he swung the deadly blade.

The assassin raised his clawed hands to block the sword, but Kaiju didn't complete the stroke. He suddenly altered the attack to a sharp diagonal cut. The long blade chopped off the ninja's hands at the wrist. The killer wailed as crimson fountains gushed from the stumps at the ends of his arms.

Kaiju delivered a backhand sweep. The katana sliced open the ninja's belly. The wounded assassin crashed to the tatamai mats, his body twitching weakly as his life bled onto the floor. Kaiju snapped the sword in a sharp downward motion, flicking the fresh blood from the blade.

Without warning, the train came to a dead stop. The occupants staggered off balance from the unexpected jolt.

Clint realized the sudden halt probably meant the ninja
had attacked O'Neal and Malone at the engine as well.

"Bastards must be all over the train," the Gunsmith
remarked.

"Nagata-sama and the *Horseman of Edo*!" Kaiju cried
out with alarm as he strode to the door, heading for the car
containing his master and the priceless gold statue.

The samurai boldly threw open the door, heedless of
any ninja traps that might be waiting for him. The
Gunsmith ran after him as Sakata and Rikko followed.
Kaiju prepared to cross over the coupling to the next car
when a ninja appeared on the platform to the warlord's
compartment.

The assassin hurled a shaken at Kaiju. The samurai
nimbly dodged the projectile. The star slammed into the
doorway just as Clint was about to cross the threshold.
The ninja drew another shaken, but he didn't live long
enough to throw it.

Kaiju leaped across the coupling, holding his katana
like a jousting knight. The slanted point of the sword bit
into the ninja's chest and plunged into the killer's heart.
The man in black bellowed in dying rage as Kaiju planted
a foot on his victim to pull his sword from the ninja's
flesh.

Another black-clad assailant suddenly swooped down
from the roof. The ninja clung to the eaves as he swung
both feet into Kaiju's chest. The kick sent the samurai
sprawling across the floor of Nagata's quarters. The ninja
plucked a throwing knife from a sheath at the nape of his
neck and prepared to hurl it at Kaiju.

Clint Adams pointed his New Line Colt at the killer's
back and squeezed off three shots. A trio of bullets struck
the ninja between the shoulder blades. The assassin's
spine snapped, and he crumbled to the platform as the

Gunsmith jumped over the coupling to the warlord's car.

Nagata knelt on the floor, his eyes staring blankly at the empty pedestal. Two dead samurai lay on the mats, but the warlord didn't seem to notice. Kaiju didn't bother to rise. He got to his knees and lowered his head until his brow touched the floor. Nagata slowly turned his head and looked at Clint Adams. Tears streaked the warlord's face.

"We have failed, Mr. Adams," he said softly. "They have taken the *Horseman of Edo*."

TWENTY-TWO

"Then we'll get it back," the Gunsmith declared. "The ninja couldn't have gotten very far."

"I'll open the gates to the car containing the horses," Kaiju announced. "We'll be able to cover more ground rapidly on horseback. Ninja skills do not include horsemanship."

"Better find out how many men we have left," Clint suggested. "And I want to talk to Culpepper if he's still alive."

"The outlaw?" Nagata frowned. "What help can he be to us, Mr. Adams."

"Culpepper was a member of the Burrows Gang," Clint explained. "Those hoot owls were famous for making stupid mistakes whenever they tried to rob a bank or a train, but to the best of my recollection, everytime a posse went after the gang it never caught up with them. That means the Burrows Gang must have learned a lot about covering up their tracks. Culpepper might be useful—if he cooperates."

"He'll cooperate, or I'll cut off his ears," Kaiju snapped.

"Let me talk to him before you start whittling on the fella," Clint urged. "I think we can make a deal with him without having to resort to violence."

"If we do not recover the *Horseman*," Nagata began,

122

"we will still have to travel to Washington D.C. Then I will pay you for your excellent work, Mr. Adams, and explain what happened to the president of the United States. It will be a sad disappointment to the leaders of both our nations, but I have no doubt that the president will believe us."

"Why?" the Gunsmith inquired. "Do you intend to commit that ritual suicide I heard about? You figure the president will be pleased to see all of you cut your guts out in front of the White House lawn?"

"Seppuku will be the only honorable course of action left to us, Mr. Adams," Nagata replied. "I do not expect you to understand this. Your culture is too different from ours. But it will be the only way we'll be able to save face and uphold the word of our emperor."

"You're right," Clint admitted. "I don't understand it. There's a lot of things I don't understand. I haven't been able to figure out why you were so opposed to the idea of contacting the army for military escort either."

"I already explained that, Mr. Adams," Nagata said crossly.

"Not to my satisfaction," Clint told him. "But we'll discuss that later. First, we have to get the statue back."

Michael O'Neal was very upset because his partner, Kelly Malone, had been killed by a ninja who entered the engine from the coal car. The silent assassin had plunged a knife into the big man's neck before the engineer even knew the enemy was present. O'Neal promptly shot the ninja in the face and killed him, but it was too late to save Kelly Malone.

"Sure'n I wish I was going with you mates," the Irishman remarked as the search party saddled their horses and prepared to hunt down the ninja thieves.

"You're needed here, Mike," the Gunsmith replied,

patting Duke's glossy black coat. "If we're not back here in two days, you take Nagata and the rest of the passengers to Washington."

"Two days?" O'Neal frowned.

"You do not need to worry about the ninja, O'Neal-san," Kaiju assured him. "They have what they wanted. They will not attack the train now."

"That's not the problem," O'Neal replied. "Two days is going to be a long wait to find out if you chaps are all right or not."

"Hopefully it won't take that long," Clint said as he slid his Springfield carbine into the saddle holster. "But if we're not back in forty-eight hours, you can be pretty sure we'll never be coming back at all."

"That's a right cheerful thing to say afore we head out after them bastards," Hal Culpepper complained, climbing onto the back of an unfamiliar mount which had formerly belonged to one of the slain samurai.

"Cheer up, Hal," the Gunsmith grinned. "We're giving you a chance to earn your freedom. You help us recover the *Horseman of Edo*, and we won't turn you over to the federal marshalls."

"And if I didn't agree to help track those ningers, or whatever you call 'em, then these sword-swingin' Japs would cut my head off."

"Look at it this way, Hal," Clint suggested. "You've got everything to lose and everything to gain."

"Great," the outlaw muttered. "I don't suppose you'd be willing to loan me a gun?"

"Surely you jest," Kaiju remarked with a wiry grin.

Sakata, the master archer, had volunteered to accompany the search party. In fact, the samurai had practically begged to go along. He felt indebted to the Gunsmith for saving his life, and he also felt he had lost face in the battle with the ninja. Clint didn't want to take any more men for the search party because that would leave the train virtually unprotected. Only four samurai had survived since the train left California, and Clint was taking two of them with him anyway.

Hal Culpepper located a set of tracks. The footprints resembled giant cloven hoof marks due to the split-toe *tabi* slippers worn by the ninja.

"All right, fellers," Culpepper announced. "This is where we start. Them ningers headed off into the forest from here. Figure there's about half a dozen of 'em. Kind'a hard to tell 'cause their tracks look so much alike. After I've been lookin' at their footprints long enough, I'll be able to tell 'em apart. Shit, I'll even be able to tell you how big each feller is and about how much he weighs."

"We're not gonna write biographies on these jaspers," Clint told him. "Just lead us to them, Hal."

"I'll do my best, Adams," the outlaw assured him. "But to tell you the truth, I ain't lookin' forward to tanglin' with them boys again."

"Maybe you're not so stupid after all," the Gunsmith said dryly as he climbed into the saddle strapped to Duke's back.

TWENTY-THREE

The four man search party made good progress for about an hour. The ninja tracks were relatively easy for Culpepper to follow. Then they came to a portion of ground which appeared to have been swept with a enormous broom. Culpepper cursed under his breath as he knelt down and stared at the ground.

"Sons of bitches are tryin' to wipe away their tracks," the outlaw announced. "Looks like they used some tree branches to sweep the ground clear of prints. It's an old Injun trick. Reckon it's an old Jap trick, too."

"Can you still read their sign?" the Gunsmith asked.

"Sure," Culpepper assured him. "Hell, the sweep marks give you a general idea which way they're headin'. Besides, there are still dents in the ground from the footprints. Sweepin' just sort of smears 'em, but if'n you look hard you can still see the tracks."

"You're doing a good job, Hal," Clint assured him. "Keep it up, and you'll be free to go wherever you want instead of getting your ass thrown in a jail cell."

"Providin' I don't get killed first," Culpepper growled.

The search party traveled another mile and a half, relying on Culpepper's ability to read sign. The ground was swept for most of that distance. Culpepper insisted they stop and asked Clint for some water. The Gunsmith handed him a canteen. The outlaw poured some water on his cupped palm and splashed it across his eyes.

"Jesus," Culpepper muttered, "these fellers surely do have discipline. I'll give them that. Never seen men sweep this much ground before. Straining my eyes so much makes me feel like I'm 'bout to wear 'em out. Still havin' trouble tellin' much from the sign 'cept for which direction they're goin'."

"That's all we really need to know," the Gunsmith assured him.

"Would be nice to know how many fellers we'll be up against," Culpepper remarked. "Hard to say about even that. Sweepin' makes that 'bout impossible cause you can't see the details of tracks well enough. Sometimes I haven't been able to see much 'cept the real heavy tracks. This statue must weigh a lot, huh? 'Bout sixty or seventy pounds, I reckon."

"That's probably about right," Clint confirmed.

"That explains the heavy prints," Culpepper stated. "Those ningers are takin' turns carryin' it."

"What worries me is whether or not they chose this area at random," Clint mused, gazing at the miles of forest surrounding them.

"This woodland environment would suit the ninja style of combat," Kaiju stated. "Trees, bushes, tall grass. Plenty of places to hide and lie in wait for us to walk into a trap."

"You reckon they'd do that instead of just takin' the statue and makin' a run with it?" Culpepper asked.

"I figure the ninja don't leave anything to chance," Clint Adams replied. "They know we have horses, and they know we want the statue as badly as they do. They'll figure we'll come after them and since they're on foot, they'll realize we might catch up with them since we've got horses.''

"But they're tryin' real hard to disguise their tracks,'' the outlaw said. "Probably figure they've wiped out their footprints, and we can't read their sign.''

"I don't think the ninja are arrogant or over confident,'' Clint insisted. "I think they'll go on the assumption that we might still trail them, and they'll be ready for us in case we do. Kaiju, you know ninja tactics better than we do. What do you figure they'll do under these circumstances?''

"Ninja are unpredictable,'' the samurai replied. "But when they know they are being pursued, they usually set traps to slow down or reduce the number of their opponents.''

"You mean 'reduce' as in *kill*?'' Culpepper asked with an uncomfortable shrug.

"Of course,'' Kaiju confirmed. "The ninja would probably use snares and weapons designed to be triggered by a pulled rope or trip wire.''

"If they can whittle us down,'' the Gunsmith remarked. "That'll put the odds in their favor. What I'm most concerned about is whether or not we're being lured into a major ambush. After all, the ninja can read maps, and they've been able to keep track of the train since we left California. Could be a whole camp of the bastards are waiting for us to walk right into their trap.''

"Jesus, Adams,'' Culpepper snorted. "You can be downright cheerful at times.''

"Everybody's gotta be good at something,'' Clint said dryly.

They followed the ninja tracks until the prints led them to the muddy shore of a small stream. Several split-toe tabi prints were clearly visible in the soft, damp earth at the edge of the water. Culpepper groaned and shook his head with dismay.

"I was a'feared somethin' like this might happen," the outlaw tracker sighed. "The ningers done found some running water. Ain't gonna be able to read their sign now. Maybe a good bloodhound could track 'em, but I sure as hell can't."

"Well," Clint began. "The ninja either headed upstream or downstream. They'll probably wade one direction or the other for a while and then cross over to the bank at the opposite side of the creek. Question is: Which way did they go?"

"Maybe I can find some sort of evidence about which way they went," Culpepper suggested, gingerly dipping a booted foot into the murky water. "Stay on the shore and let me take a looksee."

The outlaw waded to the middle of the stream and stood knee-deep in water. He peered upstream and saw nothing of interest. Then he looked downstream and saw a scrawny thornbush about fifty yards away. The bush extended from the water like a large skeletal hand. Culpepper's eyes expanded with surprise when he noticed a small patch of black cloth stuck to one of the thorny branches.

"Hold on, fellers," the outlaw announced. "I think I might have somethin' here."

Culpepper headed for the bush, water splashing up all around him. About ten feet from the bush, Culpepper cried out in fear and alarm as he suddenly stumbled and fell forward into the water. His body thrashed about wildly for a second or two, thrashing arms and legs sending jets of water above the stream. Then the outlaw lay still, his face still below the surface of the water.

The Gunsmith jumped into the stream, holding his Springfield carbine overhead as he waded toward Culpepper's inert form. Clint approached cautiously, worried about what might lie beneath the surface of the water. He moved close enough to see two wooden spikes jutting from Culpepper's back. The blood-stained, sharpened tips protruded from holes in the outlaw's shirt.

"Goddamn it," Clint growled through clenched teeth. "Culpepper's dead," he shouted to the two samurai at the shore. "They set up some sort of trip wire under the water to throw him off balance so he'd fall into a bed of sharp spikes anchored to the bottom of the stream."

"Culpep-san can no longer guide us?" Sakata inquired.

"He's dead, damn it!" Clint snapped as he waded back to shore. "Dead. Just like Hana and the sheriff back in Lawton, and God knows how many others who've been killed because of that statue of the *Horseman of Edo*. Killed because the emperor of Japan wants to make a goddamn gesture of goodwill to the president of the United States."

"You are angry, Clint," Kaiju frowned. "But surely you must appreciate the importance of our mission."

"I appreciate the fact that human life ought to mean more than a gold statue or a token of friendship from one government to another," the Gunsmith replied. "Maybe someday I'll appreciate the irony that so many people are getting killed over a peace offering from Japan to the United States. Right now, I'm tasting too much death to appreciate anything except the fact I want to stay alive."

TWENTY-FOUR

"I regard you as a friend, Clint," Kaiju began, his voice as cold and hard as frozen steel. "And I admire your courage and sense of honor. Your customs are not the same as ours. Your traditions and values are very different in many ways. Yet I must object to your remarks about the emperor who is my daimyo's master. This is offensive, Clint. Please, do not speak in such a manner again."

The Gunsmith noticed Kaiju's hand was resting on the hilt of his katana. Clint stood less than six feet away from the samurai, close enough to make a sword and a gun equal. Although the Gunsmith could probably draw and fire faster than any man alive, he wasn't sure he could beat the samurai. Kaiju wouldn't have to point and squeeze a trigger after he drew his weapon. The samurai would only have to execute one quick slash with his deadly warrior blade.

However, the Gunsmith didn't want to fight Kaiju. He wasn't angry with the samurai, and he personally liked and admired Kaiju. Clint sighed and held his open palms up in a peaceful gesture.

"I didn't mean to offend you, Kaiju," he assured the samurai. "And I don't want you to misunderstand what I'm going to say now, but it has to be said."

"I will listen," Kaiju promised, his hand still on the hilt of his sword.

"Mr. Nagata refused to even consider contacting an army base to get a cavalry escort for the *Horseman of Edo*," Clint began, lowering his fingers to the grips of his pistol. "It seemed to me that he *wanted* to tangle with the ninja and the gunmen hired by that warlord Hedora back in Japan—that is if Hedora really is to blame."

"There is no doubt that Hedora is responsible," Kaiju confirmed. "The one-eyed samurai Culpepper described must be Yamato. I explained this already."

"But you haven't explained why Nagata and Hedora are enemies," Clint replied. "They are, aren't they?"

"My daimyo and Hedora have been rivals for many years," Kaiju admitted. "Their families have fought many feuds in the past. These feuds ended under the rein of the great *shogun* Tokugawa Ieyasu, but the bitterness between the two families continued."

"In other words," Clint began. "Hedora and Nagata are picking up where their ancestors left off. That's just great. What about Nagata's duty to the emperor? Shouldn't his responsibility to deliver the *Horseman* come before an old feud with Hedora?"

"Hedora has laid down a challenge," Kaiju replied. "My master could not refuse and keep face with his ancestors. He is trying to uphold his honor to the emperor, his family, and to himself. Do you understand?"

"No," Clint confessed. "But I know that a lot of people have died trying to deliver that damn statue to the president. Doesn't seem that we should let their deaths be in vain, so let's see if we can't catch up with those ninja thieves. Agreed?"

"Indeed," Kaiju nodded. He finally took his hand from the hilt of his katana.

"Excuse me, please," Sakata began. "With Culpep-san dead, how can we find ninja now? Can you track them, Clint-san?''

"I'm not an expert tracker," the Gunsmith confessed. "But I'll have to do. Let's cross the stream here and move downstream and look for tracks at the bank.''

"Downstream?" Kaiju raised his eyebrows.

"If we don't find any there we'll look upstream," the Gunsmith declared. "But we don't split up so we can check both at the same time. There could be ninja watching us right now. If we split up that would leave one man by himself. You can bet your ass the ninja would be on him like flies on shit. We'll stick together so we don't give them any easy targets. Agreed?''

"Agreed," Kaiju nodded.

They found a number of distinct tabi footprints at the bank downstream. Even a novice tracker like the Gunsmith, could easily recognize the odd tracks. Clint whistled for Duke and grabbed the horse's reins, the Springfield carbine still in his right fist.

"I've picked up their sign," he announced to the samurai warriors. "With a little luck, I might be able to keep it.''

The Gunsmith had little trouble following the ninja tracks. The quarry was no longer making any effort to sweep the ground to wipe out footprints. This worried Clint Adams. It meant the ninja *wanted* them to follow.

"Well," the Gunsmith sighed, "we're heading into an ambush. I hope you fellas are ready for it.''

"A samurai always prepares to deal with whatever situation his karma brings," Kaiju replied as he and Sakata prepared their bows and arrows.

"Sure hope everybody's karma feels generous," the Gunsmith muttered under his breath.

The trio moved deeper into the forest, leading their horses as they cautiously approached the center of the woods. The sky was gradually getting darker. Clint and the samurai found no comfort in this. The night was the time of the ninja.

Something whistled from the branches of an oak tree. Clint felt the projectile strike the stock of his Springfield carbine. The Gunsmith glanced down at a large metal dart with a cloth tassel dangling from its end. The needle blade of the dart was lodged in the walnut stock.

Sakata raised his longbow and launched an arrow. The missile sliced through the air and rocketed upward among the tree branches. A hollow bamboo tube, two and a half feet long, fell to the base of the tree. The figure of a man in black dropped beside it, the shaft of Sakata's arrow protruding from the center of his throat.

"Be careful removing that dart, Clint," Kaiju warned, scanning the area for more aggressors.

"I know," the Gunsmith assured him, gingerly using the tips of his thumb and forefinger to pull the dart from his rifle stock. "It's poisoned. Thanks, Sakata-san."

"My pleasure, Clint-san," the samurai archer replied happily.

Another projectile sizzled from another tree. The missile narrowly missed Kaiju. It hissed past the samurai's left arm and slammed into his horse. The animal whinnied in agony and reared up on its hindlegs, an arrow buried in the beast's neck. A thrashing hoof struck Kaiju's bow, knocking it from his grasp. The horse crashed to the ground and convulsed in the dust before the poison pumped through its bloodstream to the brain.

Clint swung his Springfield toward the tree where the second assailant was lurking. He snap-aimed and fired the carbine, pumping the lever action as fast as he could. The

Gunsmith couldn't see the archer, but he hoped to flush the ninja out. Clint fired three rapid-fire rounds into the branches. Leaves spun away from the tree and bullets cracked bark from the trunk.

A black shape leaped down from the branches, a broken bow in his left fist. One of Clint's bullets had struck the weapon and shattered it. However, the ninja had already drawn a shaken from a pouch inside his jacket. Clint and Sakata aimed their weapons at the assassin.

The ninja hurled his shaken at the same instant Clint triggered his Springfield carbine. A 230 grain slug crashed into the assassin's face. His head recoiled from the impact, and his feet left the ground. The ninja was dead before his body crashed to earth.

"Jesus," the Gunsmith rasped, "that was close."

"Hai," Sakata groaned through clenched teeth as he gripped the star-shaped weapon from his flesh. "Very close, Clint-san."

The Gunsmith rushed to Sakata's side. A small crimson stain appeared on the samurai's kimono. Clint glanced about in case more ninja were about to attack, but he took a stockman's knife from his pocket and fumbled with the blade, trying to open it with just his left hand.

"We'll have to heat the blade and make an incision," the Gunsmith began. "Don't move around, Sakata. We'll suck the poison out."

"It is too late for that, Clint," Kaiju stated, gathering up his bow and arrows. "The shaken has struck too close to his heart. It is too late to help Sakata-san."

"Kaiju-san is right," Sakata said simply. "I must die soon. It is my karma, Clint-san."

"For God's sake," Clint began, frustrated and amazed by how calmly and willingly the samurai accepted his own death. "We can't just stand by and let you die."

"You can help me by letting me die with dignity," Sakata explained. "Let me die like a samurai, yes?"

"What should we do, Sakata-san?" the Gunsmith asked, reluctantly accepting the situation as well.

"I wish to die with sword in hand," Sakata replied breathlessly as he sunk to his knees. "Either in combat against the enemy, or seppuku."

"Tell me what to do," Clint said with a nod.

"I'll help Sakata-san if seppuku is the only solution," Kaiju promised. "For now, let us try to find the other ninja."

TWENTY-FIVE

The trio continued to follow the tracks of the remaining ninja as twilight fell. Clint Adams remained on foot in order to read sign. He carried the Springfield carbine in his right fist and held Duke's reins in his left. Kaiju followed, leading Sakata's horse. Sakata had tried to walk, but Clint and Kaiju had insisted he ride on the back of his mount.

"If it gets much darker I won't be able to see the ninja tracks without a lantern," Clint told Kaiju. "Even if we had a lamp, which we don't, we'd be a nice shiny target for the enemy after sundown."

"What should we do?" Kaiju inquired. "Set up camp for the night?"

"What other choice will we have?" the Gunsmith shrugged. "If we can't see where we're going, we could wind up groping through the dark and put more and more miles between ourselves and the ninja. Besides, we'd be even more likely to walk into a trap than we would be if we set up camp. Of course, we can't have a fire, and we'd better take turns sleeping."

"The ninja are probably very close," the samurai remarked. "They may be watching us at this moment."

"I know," the Gunsmith said grimly. "There's a good chance they'll make their move before dawn. We'll just have to stay alert and hope we can handle whatever they throw at us.''

"Sakata-san will not live to see the dawn," Kaiju remarked. "His breathing is labored, and he is very feverish. If we make camp for the night, Sakata-san will have to commit seppuku."

"Shit," Clint rasped. "I know it's part of your samurai customs and all that, but I still can't understand how suicide can be honorable."

"Then I can't explain it, Clint," Kaiju replied. "But please, respect our right to practice our beliefs."

'I won't try to stop him from cutting himself open,'' Clint sighed. "But forgive me if I don't want to watch him do it.''

Sakata suddenly cried out in Japanese and pointed at a bright object which shone between the trunks of two trees. The Gunsmith stared at the flash of moonlight against gold.

''*The Horseman of Edo*,'' Kaiju whispered softly.

"Yeah," Clint nodded. "But the ninja wouldn't just abandon the statue. They're trying to use it for bait to lure us into a trap.''

"I know," Kaiju agreed. "Trap or no trap, we must try to reclaim it.''

"Hold on," the Gunsmith urged. "If we charge out there we'll get ourselves killed for nothing. Let's—''

Sakata abruptly yanked the reins of his mount from Kaiju's grasp. He swatted the horse across the rump and drummed his heels against its ribs to spur the animal into a full gallop. The beast bolted forward as Sakata drew his katana from its scabbard.

Clint and Kaiju watched Sakata gallop toward the golden figure, unable to stop him. The young samurai was already doomed by the poison in his blood. If he chose to take such a bold risk, who could blame him?

Sakata galloped closer to the statue. A projectile hissed from a tree. The samurai screamed as an arrow slammed into his torso, but he remained on horseback, sword still in hand. Sakata's horse whinnied in terror as a black figure suddenly rose out of a pile of dead leaves and raised a long *yari* spear.

The ninja lunged, thrusting the lance at the man on horseback. The point of the spear stabbed into Sakata's chest. The samurai seemed to lean into the attack. The bronze tip of the lance burst through Sakata's back, blood dripping from the spearhead.

Sakata dove from the back of his mount and swung his katana in a rapid, roundhouse stroke. The long, steel blade struck the ninja lancer in the side of the neck. The assassin's head hopped from his shoulders, blood spewing from the stump of his neck.

The Gunsmith and Kaiju rushed to the cover of two tree trunks. Clint reached shelter just in time. An arrow streaked from the shadows and struck the tree as Clint ducked behind it. The Gunsmith heard the shaft of the missile vibrate like a hummingbird from the impact.

Clint could only guess where the ninja archer was hidden, but he had a general idea about which direction the arrow had come from. The Gunsmith fired two rounds at the vicinity of the enemy bowman. Another arrow whistled from the darkness and slammed into the ground less than a yard from Clint's feet.

Kaiju had seen the outline of a black shape among tree branches. The samurai notched an arrow to the string of his own bow as he watched the ninja reach for his quiver. Kaiju launched a wooden missile before the enemy archer could load his bow. The ninja shrieked as he tumbled from his roost, the samurai's arrow buried in his chest.

Clint heard the faint rustle of leaves and turned to see another ninja materialize from a cluster of bushes. The assassin held a bamboo tube to his mouth, the hollow muzzle pointed at the Gunsmith. Clint realized he couldn't aim and fire his carbine before the ninja could fire the blowgun.

The Gunsmith immediately collapsed to the ground, landing on his side, Springfield pointed in the general direction of the killer in black. A metal dart, launched from the blowgun, struck the tree above Clint's prone body. The ninja rushed forward, taking a long, sideways step as Clint triggered his carbine. The Springfield roared and the stock butt recoiled painfully against the Gunsmith's ribs.

The bullet missed the ninja by at least a foot. The killer's speed and sly movement had saved his life. Clint altered the aim of the carbine as his opponent closed in. The bamboo blowgun struck the barrel of the Springfield, parrying it away from the assassin. The wooden tube lashed out at Clint's head like a club.

The Gunsmith turned his head to the side. Bamboo cracked when it connected with the tree trunk instead of Clint's skull. The Gunsmith swiftly slashed the barrel of his carbine across the ninja's right kneecap. The assassin groaned and fell to his other knee, but he instinctively swung the bamboo tube at Clint's head once more.

The Gunsmith raised his Springfield, using the frame as a solid bar to block the ninja's cudgel. Bamboo snapped on impact. Clint quickly swung the stock of his carbine and butt-stroked the killer in the face. The ninja's head spun from the blow and his body followed. He fell on his belly, dazed and semi-conscious.

Clint couldn't afford to take any chances or show any

mercy when pitted against an enemy as determined and resourceful as a ninja. He pounced on the fallen man's back and slid the frame of his Springfield under the killer's jaw. The Gunsmith planted a knee at the small of the ninja's spine and pulled the carbine as hard as he could.

Bone cracked. The ninja moaned as blood dribbled from his lips. The Gunsmith had broken the man's back.

Clint rose to his feet, breathing hard from exertion and tension. He heard Kaiju shout a samurai battle cry and turned to see the knight-warrior pitted against another ninja. Both men had drawn swords. Steel clashed as Kaiju parried the ninja's weapon with his own blade.

The assassin tried an overhead stroke, but Kaiju's katana blocked his opponent's sword. The samurai's left leg rose swiftly and snapped a solid kick to the nerve center at the ninja's armpit. The man in black gasped and convulsed in pain. Kaiju pushed down with the blade of his sword to keep the ninja's blade immobile. Then he shoved the slanted tip of the katana forward and drove it deep into his opponent's heart.

"I think that's the last one, Kaiju," the Gunsmith announced, but he began to reload his carbine just in case he was wrong.

"Hai," the samurai replied, pulling his sword from the dead ninja's flesh. "Let us reclaim the *Horseman of Edo*, Clint."

The golden statue still stood between the trees, glowing in the moonlight like a supernatural being. Clint hadn't seen the *Horseman of Edo* since Nagata had first shown the priceless sculpture to him in California. Gold has a special majesty unmatched by any other metal, and the artwork of the statue was truly magnificent. It was indeed a beautiful and breath-taking prize which men would be willing to kill to possess.

Yet, to the Japanese delegation it meant even more than

wealth and power. It was part of their nation's heritage and culture. They were willing not only to kill for it, but die for it as well. Clint glanced down at the lifeless form of Sakata. The samurai lay beside the decapitated corpse of the ninja he had killed with his final, dying breath.

"Sakata-san died with a sword in his hand," Kaiju commented. "It is as he wished. He lived and died as a samurai with honor."

"Yeah," the Gunsmith said dryly. "I was just thinking how lucky he was. Let's get the statue and get the hell out of here."

TWENTY-SIX

Nagata was delighted and relieved when Clint Adams and Kaiju Inoshiro returned to the train with the *Horseman of Edo*. The warlord didn't seem too upset to learn that Sakata and Hal Culpepper had been killed. He ordered one of the remaining samurai to take the statue to his quarters and guard it with his life.

Life, Clint thought. A lot of lives had been lost because of that statue. Was any prize worth the sacrifice of so many brave men? The Gunsmith included the ninja in this category. The mysterious men in black were the enemy, but they were also clever and courageous. In their own way, the ninja had a code of honor which was just as binding and demanding as the samurai's Bushido.

"You have done very well, Mr. Adams," Nagata declared. "You shall receive a generous bonus for your efforts, my friend. Kaiju-san was right when he said you were the best man for the job."

"Thanks, Mr. Nagata," the Gunsmith said wearily. He was physically exhausted and sick to his stomach from all the killing and the stress of spending the night stalking and being stalked. "If you don't mind, I'd like to go to my car and get some sleep."

"Of course," the warlord agreed. "You've certainly earned a rest, Mr. Adams."

The Gunsmith made certain Duke was comfortable and

143

well fed before he headed for the caboose. He heard the
locomotive engine whistle announce that the train was
ready to move on. Clint hurried across the coupling before
the train lurched forward. He opened the door to the
caboose and stepped inside.

"Hello, Clint," Rikko greeted, kneeling on his bedroll, dressed in a kimono the color of the morning sky. "I
am glad you returned safely."

"With the *Horseman*," he added, his tone a bit more
gruff than he intended. After all, only a fool is surly with a
beautiful woman in his bed.

"My father's attitude bothers you?" she smiled. "At
times I feel the same way. He really has many good
qualities, Clint, but he also has a duty to obey the emperor. His devotion to duty can make him a bit unpleasant
at times, and like most of the elite in Japanese society, he
can be rather pompous and arrogant. Yet, my father is
basically a kind man, intelligent, generous, and very
loyal. Please, do not judge him too harshly."

"I don't mean to, Rikko," the Gunsmith assured her.
"I'm just sort of worn out and tired of having to worry if
the next shadow might try to kill me."

"You don't have to worry about that now," Rikko
assured him. "And I have something to help relax you.
See?"

She gestured toward a brass bath tub filled with hot
water. Clint blinked with surprise. Rikko picked up a
sponge and rose to her feet.

"How did you get this in here?" he asked.

"One of my father's samurai moved the bath tub in
here," Rikko explained. "I suggested that you would
have need of a pleasant, relaxing bath when you returned.
My father agreed, and he ordered the samurai to put the
tub in this car and fill it with hot water. I'm afraid the

water isn't as warm as it would have been if you had returned earlier. Please, take off your clothes and get in before it is cold."

"This is very thoughtful of you, Rikko," Clint smiled. "Thank you."

"You are welcome," she assured him. "Now take off your clothes, and I'll bathe you."

"You'll—?" the Gunsmith wasn't sure he'd heard her correctly. "Did you say you were going to give me a bath?"

"In Japan men and women often bathe together," Rikko explained. "And women bathe men. Please take off your clothes."

Hana had treated Clint to such luxury before, but he did not expect such attention from Lord Nagata's daughter. Clint decided not to look such a delightful gift horse in the mouth. He stripped out of his dusty, sweat-stained clothes and moved to the tub.

Rikko gazed over his body and smiled with approval. Clint wasn't a boy. He had seen more than forty years and survived a thousand violent encounters. Numerous scars tatooed his flesh. The Gunsmith had been wounded by bullets and knives on many occasions.

The Gunsmith's body was lean, but well muscled. He was stronger than he looked and rawhide tough. Rikko liked what she saw, and she made no attempt to hide her interest as she watched him step into the tub.

The woman untied the sash to her kimono and slipped off the robe. Clint was stunned by the beauty of her nakedness. Rikko's breasts were perfectly formed, large and firm with rigid pink nipples. Her lean waist extended to compact hips and beautiful smooth legs. Clint's penis hardened as he sat in the water, watching Rikko.

"You are a very beautiful woman," he told her.

"Thank you, Clint," she smiled. "You are beautiful, too."

Rikko dipped the sponge in the water and began to rub it over Clint's shoulders and back. His muscles relaxed, but his desire for the warlord's daughter burned like a range fire. Rikko wiped the sponge across Clint's hairy chest and scrubbed his armpits.

Clint's heart raced as Rikko's hands moved down his torso. She found his erection and gently caressed it with the sponge. Her breasts rubbed against his face. Rikko's fingers danced along his throbbing cock, rubbing him in long, slow strokes.

The Gunsmith took one of her breasts into his mouth and nibbled her. His other hand slid out of the tub and groped along her thigh. His touch moved to her buttocks and gradually shifted to the dark triangle between her lovely legs.

Clint made room in the bath tub and pulled Rikko in with him. As she straddled him, he stroked her soft, warm flesh with deft fingers and a skillful tongue. Rikko eagerly spread her thighs and steered his manhood to her womb. They moaned happily as he slid inside her.

The Gunsmith worked his member deeper, slowly rocking his loins. Rikko joined his rhythm. Clint increased the tempo. The woman trembled with pleasure and responded by bucking up and down like a wild horse. She pushed her pelvis down hard, drawing him in deeper as an uncontrollable orgasm traveled through her body.

Clint restrained his own desire for sexual release and gradually worked himself inside her again. Rikko reached her second orgasm quickly. The Gunsmith gratefully shot his hot seed into the center of her womanhood. They cried out in mutual joy, experiencing the ultimate in pleasure between a man and a woman.

"God," Clint sighed contentedly as he gently stroked her hair, "I've wanted to make love to you since the first day we met."

"I also wanted you, Clint," Rikko confessed. "I dreamed that we would make love together. It was our karma that my dream would come true."

"Well," the Gunsmith smiled. "Maybe I could learn to like the idea of karma after all."

TWENTY-SEVEN

The train traveled through the state of Texas without encountering any ninja assassins or hired gunslingers. Even the Gunsmith and Kaiju began to relax a bit as five days passed peacefully. Clint Adams certainly hoped the violence was over. Three samurai remained, and one of them spent most of his time assisting Michael O'Neal in the engine. Clint wasn't sure they could handle another full-scale attack.

He was also fearful for Rikko's safety. The Gunsmith had known many women, but few had impressed him as much as the warlord's daughter. She was beautiful and intelligent, passionate in bed and courageous in battle. He'd never been involved with a woman like Rikko before and he didn't trust himself.

The Gunsmith knew the relationship was absurd. A middle-aged drifter and a young woman of Japanese nobility. They came from two different cultures, different social levels and entirely different backgrounds. When the mission was complete—assuming they both survived—Rikko would return to Japan, and Clint Adams would take his wagon and continue to wander.

Of course, no other existence was possible for the Gunsmith. His reputation as a fast gun would hound him for the rest of his life. And Clint Adams *wanted* to die with

a gun in his hand and a bullet in his chest. He'd realized
this long ago.* It was a bizarre character trait common to
the unique breed which comprised the gunfighters of the
American West. The Gunsmith actually understood the
samurai far better than even he knew.

The train entered the Oklahoma Territory in the afternoon. O'Neal had previously announced that the steam
engine needed more water and coal for fuel. The engineer
brought the train to a halt at the town of Great Dawn
because it was equipped with a small train station and
water silo. The Gunsmith was happy to see the tiny community of Great Dawn because he hoped to get a nice,
thick beef steak. Clint was getting bored with the Japanese
diet of fish and rice. His Western-bred taste buds wanted
meat and potatoes.

The Gunsmith gazed out a window at the collection of
unimaginative, but very practical wood and adobe buildings which comprised the town of Great Dawn. The population of the Oklahoma Territory was largely Indians and
half-breeds. Folks of mixed heritage often settled there
because both the white and Indian cultures in other parts of
the country tended to give them a hard time.

Then Clint noticed something he did not expect to see.
Four men stood at the platform of the train station. Their
faces were hard with stern mouths and almond-shaped
eyes. They were dressed in dark-gray kimonos and
wooden sandals. Each carried two swords thrust in his
sash. One man stood apart from the others. He was tall and
well muscled. A black patch covered his left eye.

"Kaiju," the Gunsmith began, turning toward the
samurai. Kaiju was already staring out another window,

---

*Gunsmith #11: The One-Handed Gun

his hand instinctively gripping the hilt of his katana fighting sword.

"I know, Clint," Kaiju stated, his voice as hard as tempered steel. "It is Yamato Fujo and three of his samurai."

"Figure it's a trap?" Clint asked. "They might be planning to distract us while ninja or hired gunmen launch the real attack."

"I doubt that, Clint," Kaiju declared. "I believe the time for tricks is over. Yamato wishes to confront us directly. I believe you Americans call it a showdown, yes?"

"Maybe he wants to talk," the Gunsmith suggested.

"Samurai are warriors, not diplomats," Kaiju stated.

"But isn't Yamato a daimyo as well as a samurai?" Clint inquired. "He's sort of a sub-warlord under Hedora. That means he might be authorized to act as an ambassador for Hedora's clan."

"We've already seen what sort of tactics Hedora's people have used, Mr. Adams," Nagata announced as he approached the Gunsmith. "Do you really think he intends to discuss the matter with us now?"

The Gunsmith was surprised to see Nagata carrying a katana long sword and a short sword in his *obi* sash. The warlord had never armed himself before now. Clint frowned. If the portly, middle-aged Nagata planned to take on the one-eyed samurai, then Nagata was sure as hell tempting fate—or karma.

"I'm saying we should talk to him before we jump to any conclusions," Clint explained. "Maybe since the ninja failed to stop us, Yamato will be willing to negotiate an agreement in order to save face for himself and Hedora."

"The terms can't be negotiated," Nagata insisted. "We have to deliver the *Horseman of Edo* to the president, and Yamato intends to claim it and return it to Hedora in Japan. There is no way we can reach a compromise. After all, we can't cut the statue in half, Mr. Adams.''

"I realize that," the Gunsmith assured him. "But Yamato might be willing to deal with us in order to get our silence. I'm sure Hedora doesn't want the emperor to know he tried to steal the *Horseman*. What the hell harm can it do to just talk to Yamato?"

"Very well, Mr. Adams," Nagata agreed. "We'll try diplomacy—if Yamato doesn't simply attack as soon as we set foot outside this train. May I suggest you be prepared to fight, nonetheless."

"Don't worry about that," Clint replied. "I'll do what has to be done, but there's already been a lot of blood shed, and if we can avoid any more, I'd rather not have to kill anyone else."

"Don't hope for that too hard, Mr. Adams," Nagata warned. "Because that's one wish which might not come true."

Kaiju and Clint Adams stepped from the train first. Yamato and his three samurai stared at them, but neither spoke nor gestured to acknowledge their presence. The men in the gray kimonos didn't advance, so the Gunsmith kept his fingers off the grips of his Colt, although his hand hung near the holstered revolver.

Nagata and his other two samurai emerged from the train and joined the others on the platform. Yamato stepped forward and bowed. The gesture was formally polite, neither a deep bow of respect or a curt nod of simple acknowledgement. Nagata returned the gesture with an identical bow.

"*Konnichi-wa, Nagata-san,*" the one-eyed samurai greeted.

"*Konnichi-wa,*" Nagata replied simply.

They conversed in rapid Japanese. Clint was totally baffled concerning the conversation. The tone seemed angry, but the Gunsmith had previously noticed that the voice inflection in Japanese is different than English. It was difficult to tell what was going on just from the sound of the words.

Clint tried to read something in the facial expressions of Nagata and the samurai. It was a waste of time. The Japanese would make great poker players, the Gunsmith decided. Nagata and Yamato remained roughly eight feet apart; their postures were straight and their eyes betrayed nothing. When either man listened to the other speak, his mouth formed a straight line without the slightest hint of a smile or a frown.

Then the Gunsmith noticed three men had joined them on the train station platform. The trio carried shotguns and each wore a gunbelt. One man also had a spare revolver thrust in his belt. Clint's hand draped the grips of his modified Colt, fearing the trio might be hired gunmen. Maybe Yamato had lured them into a trap after all.

However, the Gunsmith quickly moved his hand when he saw the copper badges pinned to the shirts of the three men. The Japanese also noticed the lawmen. Their conversation ceased abruptly, and Nagata turned to face them.

"May I help you, gentlemen?" the warlord inquired.

"I'm Sheriff Spotted Elk," one of the lawmen replied. "These are my deputies. We've been kinda keepin' an eye on the fellers waitin' for the train to arrive. Didn't reckon they was just passin' through town."

Spotted Elk was a tall lean man with copper-colored skin and a hawkbill nose. Clint guessed he was probably half-Cherokee. Spotted Elk may have been a former Confederate soldier in the Cherokee Rifle Regiment. A lot of

Indian and half-breed veterans migrated to Oklahoma after the War Between the States.

"This is not a violation of American law," Yamato stated in a gruff, hard voice.

"No law against you fellers bein' here," Spotted Elk agreed. "And there ain't nothin' wrong with you standin' here at the train station talkin' to each other neither, but you don't look like you're havin' a friendly conversation. I figure maybe you fellers might draw them sabers and start to whittlin' on each other. Can't say that I'd take kindly to that."

"We are discussing a matter of diplomacy concerning Japan and the United States," Nagata explained. "Although, I must admit we disagree."

"Disagree most strongly," Yamato added curtly.

"Well, I'll tell you boys somethin'," the sheriff began. "This is a nice quiet little town. We hold with no gun-fightin' in the streets of Great Dawn, and I don't want no sword fightin' neither. You wanta settle anythin' with a gun or a blade, you get the hell outta our town and have your duelin' elsewhere."

"Very well," Nagata assured him. "We've already finished our discussion for now anyway. Correct, Yamato-san?"

"Until morning, Nagata-sama," the one-eyed samurai confirmed with a nod.

Yamato turned sharply and walked from the platform, followed by his three samurai henchmen.

TWENTY-EIGHT

The Gunsmith waited until the sheriff and his deputies left the platform. Then he turned to Nagata.

"Mind telling me what you fellas said?" Clint asked.

"Yamato explained that he was here in America to carry out a mission for his master, Hedora," Nagata explained. "Of course, this was something we already knew. I told him we realized Hedora had sent the ninja to steal the *Horseman of Edo*. I also informed him that we were already aware that he was in command of the thieves here in America."

"Did he deny it?" Clint asked.

"No," Nagata answered. "Yamato claimed that the *Horseman of Edo* is the rightful property of Lord Hedora. His master sent him to reclaim the statue and he is bound by the code of Bushido to obey Hedora's order."

"But you said the *Horseman* was the property of the emperor of Japan," the Gunsmith reminded him.

"That is correct," Nagata confirmed. "Hedora has no claim to it. Of course, Yamato does not believe this. He demands that I surrender the *Horseman* to him. Naturally, I refused."

"What did Yamato say about that?"

"He said it was his duty to get the *Horseman*," Nagata replied. "Yamato insisted that his mission was more important than the life of any individual person. More

154

important than his life or mine. I informed him that I felt the same about my mission to deliver the *Horseman* to the president. Then I followed your suggestion and told Yamato if he would stop trying to steal the statue and allow us to complete our mission for the emperor, then his master would not lose face because we would take a vow of silence and promise never to tell of Hedora's efforts to steal the *Horseman*."

"I take it Yamato didn't accept the offer," Clint guessed.

"No," the warlord sighed. "Yamato repeated his claim that the *Horseman of Edo* belonged to Hedora. He accused me of being a liar and a coward. Yamato then challenged me to a duel."

"Did you accept?" the Gunsmith asked.

"I told him I would have to consider whether or not I would accept the challenge," Nagata explained. "You may not believe me, Mr. Adams, but I would have agreed to the duel if only my life was at stake."

"I believe you," Clint assured him. "But you have a responsibility to deliver the *Horseman* to the president."

"True," Nagata nodded. "But my daughter Rikko could continue the mission if I died. That is why I brought her on this dangerous assignment. Perhaps Yamato's challenge is an omen. It may be my karma to face him in a duel of honor."

"I don't mean to be disrespectful, Mr. Nagata," the Gunsmith began. "But you said this Yamato character is supposed to be one of the best swordsmen in Japan. Do you think you'd have a chance against him?"

"There is always a chance," Nagata replied. "Yamato is a far better swordsman than I. He is younger and faster. To be honest, I was never an exceptional swordsman. I was always a better scholar and diplomat than a warrior."

"Nagata-sama," Kaiju said urgently. "Please, let me act as your champion. I will duel with Yamato instead. He represents Hedora. I can represent you."

"I appreciate your loyalty and courage, Kaiju-san," Nagata said fondly. "But Yamato made the challenge personally, and he made it in no one's name except his own. He is a daimyo and thus it would be an insult to ask him to duel with someone of lesser rank. It would also be considered an act of cowardice on my part."

"I don't understand why you'd even consider fighting Yamato under the circumstances," Clint remarked. "Even if you got lucky, and you managed to kill him, would that stop the other three samurai from continuing to try to prevent us from reaching Washington?"

"It probably would," Nagata answered. "Yamato is the only member of his band who speaks English. Some of his ninja also spoke English, but apparently they're all dead. The lesser samurai would not be able to function effectively in this country. They would probably commit seppuku to try to cleanse themselves of their failure."

"You fellas sure have tough rules," the Gunsmith sighed. "I'm sure you realize Yamato would probably win if you accept the duel."

"I know," Nagata admitted. "But I might be able to catch him off guard. Even if he wins, I may be able to execute one final thrust or slash and take him with me to the next incarnation."

"That's a long shot, and you know it," Clint told him. "And don't tell me it's karma for you to agree to fight Yamato. That will be your decision, not an act of fate."

"Yes, Mr. Adams," the warlord said stiffly. "*My* decision, not yours. I have until dawn to make that decision. Frankly, it is none of your concern, Mr. Adams."

"The hell it isn't," the Gunsmith said gruffly. "I'm

mixed up in this mess along with everybody else on this train. Your decision will affect everybody who has risked his or her life because of you and that gold statue. So you go ahead and make your decision, Mr. Nagata. Just be sure you consider everything involved and not just accept Yamato's challenge because your family and the Hedora clan have an old feud."

"That has nothing to do with this," Nagata snapped.

"That's right," Clint agreed, "and I sure hope you'll remember that."

"Thank you for your advice, Mr. Adams," the warlord said dryly. "Now, if you don't mind, I want to meditate and consider what choice of action to take."

Nagata climbed into the passenger compartment of the train. Kaiju turned to the Gunsmith.

"Do not judge my master harshly, Clint," the samurai urged. "He is a wise man, and he will make the right decision. Whatever the outcome, we will simply have to accept it."

"I can if you can," Clint commented.

"Is there some hidden meaning to your words?" Kaiju inquired.

"You said that the way of the samurai is doomed," Clint explained. *The Horseman of Edo* is a gift to the president to try to increase diplomatic bonds between Japan and the Western world. Won't that hasten the end of the samurai class?"

"You think I would turn against my master?" Kaiju said fiercely. "I would never dishonor my ancestors, my lord or myself by such treachery."

"I know you wouldn't, Kaiju," Clint assured him. "And that's why this must be very hard for you."

"I'm being forced to help end a way of life which has been part of my heritage for centuries," Kaiju stated softly. "A way of life which means everything to me. Yet, the code of Bushido requires I do this. Ironic that my own principles are being used to make me do what I fear most."

"Sometimes it seems like the world doesn't make much sense," the Gunsmith sighed. "Right now all I know for sure is I want to find myself a steak and potatoes dinner."

"Good luck," the samurai smiled. "I hope you can find something in life that you want."

"Reckon that's up to karma," Clint shrugged.

TWENTY-NINE

The Gunsmith found a cafe in Great Dawn and ordered the biggest, thickest steak the cook could fit in a skillet. Clint shuffled all other thoughts to the back of his mind and concentrated on enjoying the meal.

Clint paid for his meal and allowed himself the luxury of purchasing a good cigar. Twilight had fallen. The Gunsmith gazed up at the smattering of stars in the evening sky as he struck a match on the supporting post to the porch roof and lit his cigar. Roughly eight hours until dawn. He wondered what Nagata would decide to do.

If the warlord accepted the challenge to face Yamato, he would almost certainly be killed. That sure as hell wouldn't make their job any easier. What would happen if Nagata refused to duel with the one-eyed samurai? Clint couldn't see how the warlord's refusal could make matters worse.

"Help! Please!" a woman's voice cried softly from an alley between the cafe and the general store. "Somebody, help me!"

The Gunsmith dashed to the mouth of the alley, hand poised on the butt of his revolver. He peered inside and saw a burly man dressed in dirty denim and a sweat-stained stetson holding a woman against the wall of the store. She was young, with long black hair and dark

159

Indian features. The woman gasped and weakly cried out for help as the man pinned her against the wall.

"Let her go," the Gunsmith demanded, drawing his Colt from leather.

He entered the alley. The man released the woman. She didn't even glance at Clint as she bolted to the opposite end of the alley, and vanished around a corner. Oh, well, Clint thought. Maybe she'll send me a thank-you card later.

Suddenly, another man appeared from a rain barrel at the wall of the cafe. The Gunsmith barely saw a blur of movement before the ambusher seized his wrist and adroitly twisted the double-action Colt from Clint's grasp.

"Shit," the Gunsmith rasped as he rammed a knee between the man's legs.

The aggressor howled in agony and stumbled away from Clint, both hands grasping his battered genitals. Clint quickly hit him with a right cross to the jaw, followed by a left hook and an uppercut to the solar plexus. The fellow doubled over and began to sink to his knees, wheezing like an overworked old plow horse.

Clint raised his fist to hit his opponent again, but the other man grabbed his arm and spun him around. A fist crashed into the Gunsmith's face. The blow knocked him backward into a wall. The burly assailant charged forward and raised a boot, prepared to stomp Clint's guts hard enough to push them out of his mouth.

The Gunsmith dodged the foot. His opponent's boot stamped the wall forcibly. Clint's left fist jabbed twice, tagging the attacker on the point of the chin and the tip of his nose. The man's head bobbed from the stinging punches, and Clint swung a hard right for his jaw.

A muscular forearm blocked the Gunsmith's punch and the brute rammed a fist to Clint's stomach. A left hook sent Clint staggering into his first opponent who had just dragged himself up from all fours. The Gunsmith didn't give the man enough time to clear his head. Clint clapped both palms to the man's ears. The ambusher bellowed in pain as his head seemed to explode. He clasped both hands to the sides of his skull, and Clint kicked him in the testicles again. This time the man crumbled to the ground unconscious.

Strong fingers seized Clint from behind. He lashed out with an elbow, slamming it across the burly aggressor's jaw. The big man swayed, caught off guard by the tactic. Clint hit him again with a left and an overhead right which planted his knuckles squarely on the bridge of his opponent's nose. Blood squirted from the man's nostrils.

"Goddamn you, Adams!" the ambusher snarled as he lowered his head and charged like a ram.

The Gunsmith could hardly believe anyone could be so stupid. He let the brute close in and then whipped a knee under the idiot's jaw. The blow straightened his opponent's back and set him up for a right cross from the Gunsmith. The man's face danced from the impact of Clint's knuckles, and his knees buckled weakly.

Clint clasped both hands together and swung them like an axe, chopping the larger man under the heart. The brute doubled over with a groan. Clint grabbed his opponent by the back of the neck and his belt. He hauled the ambusher head first into the nearest wall. At last, the burly man fell in a senseless heap.

"Very good, Mr. Adams," a gruff voice declared. "I thought you might be too much for those two fools to cope with."

The Gunsmith turned to see Yamato Fujo at the mouth of the alley. A stocky man dressed in a shabby jacket and a Montana-peak hat stood beside the samurai. He scowled at the Gunsmith and pointed a sawed-off Greener shotgun at Clint. The Gunsmith turned to the other end of the alley. Two of Yamato's samurai were stationed there, hands poised on the handles of their swords.

"Glad I didn't disappoint you, fella," Clint said, raising his hands in surrender.

"I'll disappoint you to death, Adams," the shabby man in the Montana-peak hat snarled. "You and them bastards on the train done kil't my entire gang, 'cept for Clem and Yancy. Ain't so sure they'll be right in the head after the way you whupped 'em."

"Then you must be Jake Burrows," Clint remarked. "The way I hear, a fella can't be right in the head to join your gang in the first place."

"I oughta blow your head off, you no-count puke eater," Burrows growled, aiming his shotgun at the Gunsmith's face.

"Yamato-san wouldn't like that," Clint remarked calmly. "You didn't go to all this trouble to take me alive just to let Burrows work off some frustrations, did you, Yamato-san?"

"You are very acute, Mr. Adams," the one-eyed samurai said with a smile.

"What's cute about him?" Burrows asked, confused by the samurai's remark.

"Your ignorance is almost painful, Mr. Burrows," Yamato sighed. "Pick up Mr. Adams' gun. We'll return it to him after we've discussed business."

"What?" the outlaw glared at Yamato. "You ain't serious. This here's the Gunsmith! If'n he hadn't been on that train, my men would have gotten that gold statue for you by now, Mr. Yamato."

"Perhaps," the samurai mused. "But I would prefer that Mr. Adams be a valuable ally than a formidable foe.

But I could not expect Mr. Adams to consider changing sides if he wasn't assured that he would be allowed to live regardless of his decision. Please, come with us, Mr. Adams. You have my word as a daimyo and a samurai warrior that you shall not be harmed.''

"Unless I refuse to accompany you to wherever we're going?" the Gunsmith inquired.

"We've already spent too much time in this alley," Yamato said, his tone suggesting he was getting annoyed. "If you do not come with us, we'll be forced to kill you."

"Well," Clint shrugged, "I reckon I can't refuse an invitation like that."

The Gunsmith was escorted to a tent at the outskirts of town. It was roughly the size of a cavalry officer's tent. A rope corral contained several horses, and candles or lamps were lit inside the tent. Yamato signaled for the group to stop.

He barked a curt order in a loud voice. To the Gunsmith's surprise, two black-clad masked figures suddenly appeared from the surrounding shadows. The ninja carried swords, bows and arrows and, no doubt, an assortment of devilish hidden weapons as well.

"These two ninja are the last remaining members of the Muzuku Clan," Yamato explained. "They are not happy with you and the others on the train for having killed so many of their brethren. I called them forward to instruct them that I forbid any aggression to be taken against you this night—either at my camp or when you leave."

"Thanks for your protection," Clint said. "Even if it is just for the night."

"That will be for you to decide, Mr. Adams," Yamato replied as he led the Gunsmith into the tent.

The interior was carpeted with tatamai mats and decorated with brass incense burners, paper lanterns, and silk screens. The men took off their footgear before entering the tent. Even Jake Burrows removed his boots. Yamato walked to the center of the room and knelt on the mat, placing his katana beside him.

"Mr. Adams," Yamato began. "I feel I should explain that we do not feel any resentment toward you. You are, after all, a mercenary. The importance of the *Horseman of Edo* does not truly matter to you. Nagata is paying you to help escort the statue, but it is the rightful property of Hedora-sama."

"I'm not a mercenary," Clint explained. "Nagata claims the *Horseman* belongs to the emperor of Japan."

"The *Horseman of Edo* was the property of the Hedora family for many generations," Yamato declared. "It was confiscated by the Imperial Treasury. My master still regards the *Horseman* as his property. I am a samurai. I know nothing of politics, but I understand my duty to my master."

"So you figure you have to carry out your mission," Clint sighed. "Everybody feels that way. Everybody is bound by honor and the code of Bushido. I know all about that, Yamato-san."

"You've heard about it," the samurai said. "But you don't understand. You and Mr. Burrows are hired assassins. Honor is not your concern. Profit is all that matters to you. Nagata is paying you to protect the *Horseman of Edo*. I will pay you twice as much to give the statue to me. A simple task, yes?"

"Maybe," the Gunsmith replied. "But you've misjudged me, Yamato-san. I'm not a thief, and I won't steal the statue for you. Honor isn't exclusive only to you Japanese, fella. I gave my word to Nagata and Kaiju. That means I've got an obligation to them. You understand?"

"I see," Yamato nodded. "I apologize, Mr. Adams. I

meant no offense. Mr. Burrows will give you your pistol, and you may leave.''

"Like hell!" Burrows snapped, raising his shotgun. Clint found himself staring into the twin muzzles of the cut-down Greener.

"Burrows!" Yamato barked. "Put down your weapon. I promised Mr. Adams he would not be harmed."

"I didn't promise nothin'," the outlaw replied. "When you got yourself an enemy like the Gunsmith, you don't play games with him. I'm gonna kill this—"

Yamato suddenly rose from the floor in a swift, yet graceful motion. His kimono seemed to float into the air. A flash of metal whirled under Jake Burrows' chin. The outlaw's head vanished. Clint heard it softly strike the mats as he watched fountains of crimson jet from the man's severed neck.

Jake Burrows' decapitated corpse slumped to the floor. Yamato calmly wiped the blade of his sword on the dead man's shirt before returning it to the scabbard. The samurai plucked the modified Colt revolver from Burrows' belt and returned it to the Gunsmith.

"You didn't unload this gun," Clint remarked. "What's to stop me from killing you and your friends now?"

"Your honor, Mr. Adams," Yamato smiled.

"Reckon you're right," Clint shrugged as he slid his pistol into leather. "Sure be an easy way to solve some problems, but I'm not sure it would be the right way."

"Right and wrong are often difficult to recognize," Yamato commented. "Nagata and I are enemies, although we have no personal reason to be against each other. We both think what we do is right, and we're both driven by a code of honor which dictates our action. Like soldiers who kill total strangers on the battlefield, we face a situation which is beyond our control. Perhaps neither of us is right. Perhaps neither is wrong.''

"I figure if a man follows his principles," Clint mused, "he's being true to himself. Maybe that's the best way to determine what right and wrong are."

"I've enjoyed our conversation, Mr. Adams," Yamato said sincerely. "I hope I won't be forced to kill you, but please understand, I shall do so if I must."

"I'll do the same to you if I have to," the Gunsmith grinned. "Sort of like the gunfighter's unofficial motto—'nothing personal, just business.' "

"I'm glad you understand," Yamato nodded. "Return to the train, Mr. Adams. Tomorrow we shall see what Nagata decides to do. After all, events and lives will be in the hands of karma."

"And our individual skill with gun or sword," Clint Adams added.

"Of course," the samurai confirmed. "That too."

THIRTY

Clint Adams returned to the train. Michael O'Neal met him at the platform of the train station. The engineer wearily waved at the Gunsmith and took a pouch of tobacco and rolling papers from his pocket. O'Neal constructed a cigarette and struck a match.

"What happened to you?" he asked, noticing a bruise on Clint's jaw.

"You wouldn't believe me if I told you," the Gunsmith replied. "Is the train ready to continue on to Washington?"

"Well," O'Neal began, drawing deeply from his cigarette. "They had plenty of water in the silo, but no coal or wood. According to the map, there's another train station about thirty miles north. We'll have to get the rest of our fuel there. Should be able to make the trip on what we've got right now. Of course, I'm not sure *all* of us will live to make the journey."

"You think Nagata will agree to duel with Yamato?" Clint inquired.

"I don't know," the Irishman shrugged. "But if he does fight Yamato, I figure the one-eyed bloke will take him."

"Could be," Clint said, but he recalled Yamato's speed and accuracy with a blade when he decapitated Jake

Burrows. O'Neal was right. Nagata was no match for the one-eyed samurai.

"What do you reckon will happen tomorrow?" O'Neal asked.

"I don't know," the Gunsmith confessed. "Guess we'll all find out in the morning."

"Yeah," the Irishman sighed, dropping his cigarette and grinding it under the toe of his boot. "I suppose frettin' about it won't change anything."

"Not a thing," Clint agreed. "Get some sleep, Mike."

Yamato and his trio of samurai appeared at the platform of the train station roughly half an hour after sunup. Nagata and his men were waiting for them. Clint Adams stood by the train. He had no idea what would happen next, or what he'd be required to do. Karma, he thought. Just wait and see what fate throws at you.

"Nagata-sama," Yamato began. "Have you decided to accept my challenge?"

"I considered the matter very carefully," Nagata answered. "My duty to the emperor and to the lives of my people on this train must take priority over personal offenses. So I must respectfully refuse to duel with you."

"I expected as much," Yamato smiled thinly. "The Nagata family has always been noted for their lack of personal honor and their highly developed sense of cowardice."

Kaiju and the other samurai under his command stiffened, their hands moving to the hafts of their swords. Nagata uttered a curt command in Japanese. Reluctantly, his men relaxed.

"Your insults are meant to cause rash action, Yamato-san," Nagata declared. "Since I am aware of this, I will not play the fool and respond as you desire."

"Cowards always have excuses not to fight, Nagata-sama," Yamato replied simply.

Suddenly, one of Nagata's samurai screamed in uncontrollable anger and drew his katana from its scabbard. He charged forward, sword held in a two-fisted grip. One of Yamato's samurai stepped forward and reached for his weapon. Nagata's swordsman struck before the other man could draw his katana. Steel chopped into Yamato's samurai's head, cutting him from the crown of his head to the bridge of his nose. Blood poured from the man's split face as he crumbled to the platform.

"*Eya, Hara-san!*" Nagata shouted as he seized the wrist of his emotional samurai. "No! This outburst is a disgrace to my family! You are rude and undisciplined, Hara-san!"

The man stepped away from Nagata and fell to his knees, placing his katana on the platform. He uttered something in Japanese. Nagata turned to Kaiju and asked him a question. The samurai commander nodded in reply. The Gunsmith watched Yamato and the other swordsmen in gray. They did not seem distressed that one of their comrades had been killed. In fact, they appeared to be pleased with whatever Nagata had said.

Kaiju Inoshiro slowly drew his katana. He stepped next to the man who knelt on the platform and raised his sword. The disgraced samurai chanted as he took a knife from his sash. He held the blade to his own abdomen and shoved it in hard.

Clint watched in fascinated horror as the samurai stabbed himself and dragged the knife across his belly. The man's face contorted in pain, but he did not cry out. He continued the cut until his guts poured out of the terrible wound.

Kaiju swung his katana. The edge of his sword caught Hara across the back of the neck. His severed head rolled across the platform as blood pumped from the stump of his neck. Kaiju snapped his wrist and flicked the man's blood from his sword.

"My God," the Gunsmith whispered, stunned by what he had witnessed.

"Hara-san died well," Yamato declared. "He did you honor as well as himself, Nagata-sama."

"Hai," Nagata nodded. "But I still must apologize for his conduct and the death of your man, Yamato-san. However, I still must refuse to duel with you."

The roar of a shotgun drew everyone's attention to the three figures who hurried toward the platform. Sheriff Spotted Elk and his deputies were armed to the teeth and clearly horrified by what had taken place at the train station.

"Goddamn you crazy bastards!" the sheriff exclaimed. "I told you I didn't want no swordfightin' in my town and just look at what you fellers done. Cuttin' off each other's heads, for crissake!"

"I'm afraid there was a misunderstanding, sheriff," Nagata explained.

"You fellers kill each other, and you call it a 'misunderstanding'?" Spotted Elk glared at the warlord. "I want you fellers to get out of Great Dawn right now! I want you the hell out of here before you have another 'misunderstanding' which might get somebody in town killed as well."

"We'll have to finish our business later, Nagata-sama," Yamato stated. He turned to the Gunsmith. "May I suggest that Mr. Adams remain here in town? None of this really concerns him."

"Mr. Adams is free to make his own decisions," Nagata said.

"I signed on with your crew," the Gunsmith told him. "I'll see my job through to the end."

"I don't care what you folks do so long as you don't do it in Great Dawn," the sheriff snapped. "Now get back on the train and get the hell outta town!"

"My men and I did not arrive on the train, sheriff," Yamato declared. "We shall pull down our tent and move on, however, so you need not concern yourself. We are going, sir."

"See to it," Spotted Elk snapped. "The rest of you jaspers get onboard that goddamn train."

"Of course," Nagata promised. "I apologize for this disturbance, sheriff."

"The hell with your apologizing," Spotted Elk replied. "And take those dead bodies with you."

"But one of them belongs to Yamato-san," Nagata explained, watching the enemy trio walk from the platform.

"I don't care," the sheriff insisted. "I'm not gonna have a cut-up corpse carried through town where women and children might see it."

"Very well," the warlord sighed. "We'll take care of the bodies."

"Good," the sheriff grunted. "Say, aren't you Clint Adams, the Gunsmith?"

"I'm Clint Adams," the Gunsmith replied simply.

"What the hell are you doin' with these lunatics?" Spotted Elk inquired.

"How the hell do I know?" Clint said with a shrug.

THIRTY-ONE

The train left the town of Great Dawn and headed north. Clint Adams finally had an opportunity to tell Nagata and Kaiju about his unexpected meeting with Yamato the night before. The warlord and the samurai were only mildly surprised and not at all alarmed by the story.

"Perhaps our troubles are finally over," Nagata mused with a smile. "Yamato killed the outlaw leader so I assume he doesn't have any more gunmen left on his payroll."

"He killed Jake Burrows in order to save my life," Clint commented.

"No, Clint," Kaiju corrected. "Yamato killed Burrows to save face. He did it to uphold his honor after promising you that you wouldn't be harmed."

"Well, he still kept Burrows from blowing my head off with a shotgun. To tell the truth, I started out on this little trip thinking the ninja were shadowy villains, and Hedora and Yamato were unprincipled bastards. But now, I kind of admire the ninja, and Yamato has turned out to be an honorable man who saved my life. I can't just dismiss that."

"What are you trying to say, Mr. Adams?" Nagata asked.

"I don't like the idea of having to kill Yamato," Clint

admitted. "And I won't do it unless I have to in order to save my life or the life of one of you."

"Fair enough," Nagata assured him. "But I doubt that we'll have to worry about Yamato again. From what you told us about Yamato's camp, he and his samurai are traveling on horseback and burdened with a large tent. They can't possibly travel as quickly as this train. You also said that Yamato claimed the two ninja you saw were the last members of their clan. As long as we keep moving and don't stop for an extended period at any single spot, Yamato will not be able to catch up with us. Yes?"

"I wouldn't bet on that," the Gunsmith replied. "Every time we begin to figure we've seen the last of these fellas, they wind up coming out of the woodwork with weapons drawn."

"The situation is different now," Nagata declared.

"I hope you're right," Clint sighed. "Since Hara commited suicide, you've only got two samurai left, including Kaiju. We're not in very good shape to handle an organized assault."

"Yamato isn't in very good shape to launch one," the warlord said wearily. "Relax, Mr. Adams."

"How about you, Kaiju?" Clint asked. "Do you figure we can just relax now?"

"I would not contradict the wisdom of my master," Kaiju replied. "But I am a samurai, and thus I must always be ready for trouble. I never relax and never ignore my duty."

"Even when your duty means you have to chop off the head of one of your own men?" the Gunsmith asked dryly.

"I assure you Kaiju-san found no pleasure in decapitating Hara-san today," Nagata said, his voice containing an edge of anger. "Hara-san asked permission to commit seppuku after his rash actions brought disgrace to himself and to me. I granted him permission to cleanse himself by an honorable death.''

"Why?'' Clint asked. "Why didn't you tell him not to kill himself?''

"Because honor means more than life, Mr. Adams,'' Nagata explained. "Hara-san was a samurai, and he died as wished. I asked Kaiju-san to strike off his head. This was an act of mercy by myself and by Kaiju-san, who did not have to accept this unpleasant task. Otherwise, Hara-san would have suffered most terribly for many hours before he died. Do you understand?''

"No,'' the Gunsmith confessed, "and I don't think I want to.''

The train reached a railroad depot that afternoon. It was a remote station, consisting of little more than a small wooden house, a water silo, and a barn which had been converted into a storage area for coal and cords of wood. O'Neal brought the train to a halt.

Clint Adams and Fukuda-san, the last samurai under Kaiju, climbed from the train to help O'Neal load coal and wood into the bins of the locomotive. The pair approached the house as O'Neal moved to the side of the engine to urinate. The Gunsmith noticed a curtain move in a window, but no one emerged from the house. Maybe the residents were uncertain of what to make of the samurai, dressed in a robe and carrying two swords. Or maybe . . . .

Something bolted from the window. Fukuda-san shrieked as an arrow slammed into his chest. The samurai fell in a quivering heap as the Gunsmith drew his double-action Colt and squeezed off two rapid-fire rounds at the house.

Clint dashed to the cover of an iron coal car. Something

struck the metal cart. Clint glanced over the rim and caught a glimpse of a black shape on the roof of the house. The ninja reached for another arrow to reload his bow.

The report of a rifle echoed from the engine of the train. O'Neal had obviously grabbed his weapon and joined the fight. The ninja on the roof dropped his bow and tumbled from the top of the house, landing on the ground hard, raising a cloud of dust on impact.

Silence followed. Nearly a minute passed as the Gunsmith crouched behind the coal car and waited. He wondered if one of his shots had made a lucky hit, and the ninja inside the house was already dead. Clint wasn't curious enough to stroll out into the open to find out.

"Hold your fire!" a voice shouted in a high-pitched plea. "For God's sake, don't shoot!"

A middle-aged black man, dressed in denim overalls and long-john undershirt, stumbled from the house. He held his hands in the air as he nervously approached. Clint leaned around the edge of the coal car and aimed his Colt at the window where the first arrow had been launched.

"Don't shoot!" the man repeated. "Jesus Lord, don't shoot me!"

"Head for the train," the Gunsmith shouted. "We don't want to hurt you, and if the ninja wanted to kill you, you'd be dead already."

"What do we do now, Clint?" O'Neal's voice called from the locomotive.

"Stay behind cover," Clint replied. He tried to put himself in the ninja's position. What would he do if he was holed up in a house?

And why had the ninja released the black man?

"He's trying to distract us," the Gunsmith whispered through clenched teeth. "Mike, fire a couple rounds at the front door. Keep the bastard busy."

"Right," the Irishman confirmed.

The Gunsmith waited for the crack of O'Neal's rifle before he broke cover. Clint dashed to the house, his back arched in a half-crouch. He dove forward and rolled to the side of the building. Staying low, he crept under the sill of a window and moved to the rear of the house.

The ninja was waiting for him around the corner.

Clint saw a blur of motion and felt something strike his forearm hard enough to knock the Colt revolver from his grasp. The ninja held some sort of stick-weapon in his fist. It whirled and hit Clint's triceps. He ducked in time to avoid a stroke to his head. Wood struck the corner of the building hard.

The Gunsmith dove into his opponent. Both men fell to the ground, but the ninja held onto his weapon and lashed it across Clint's back, striking him between the shoulder blades. The damn thing was flexible. The ninja flogged Clint again and again, clubbing him painfully with his odd weapon.

The Gunsmith tried to roll away from his opponent and lashed out a kick at the ninja. Pain shot up from his shin as the assassin in black struck him with the stick-weapon once again. The ninja rose to his feet and held the device in both hands. Clint finally got a clear look at the weapon. It was just a pair of sticks connected by a short piece of chain. A simple contraption, but Clint had no doubt the ninja could beat him to death with that damn thing.

The killer raised his weapon to launch another attack. Clint's left hand clawed at the ground, gathering up a fistful of dirt as his right hand reached under his shirt. He hurled the dirt at the ninja's face. The weapon struck the ground near Clint's head as the ninja swung blindly, trying to wipe his eyes with his free hand.

Clint drew his New Line Colt as the assassin raised his weapon once more. The Gunsmith fired the diminutive pistol, blasting three rounds upward into the ninja's throat and jawbone. Two .22 caliber slugs ripped open the assassin's windpipe while the third burned through the hollow of his jaw and pierced the roof of his mouth. The bullet came to rest in the ninja's brain. He staggered awkwardly, dropped his sticks and dropped dead beside the Gunsmith.

Clint slowly got to his feet, his muscles painfully sore from the beating he'd received from the ninja's weapon. Later he would learn the device was called a *nunchaku*. The Gunsmith found his .45 caliber Colt and returned it to its holster before he slid the little "belly gun" to its usual place.

He shuffled around the building. O'Neal had ventured away from the train, Winchester in his fists. Kaiju had also advanced, armed with his kyujutsu bow and arrows. Even Lord Nagata had left the train.

"Did you get 'im, Clint?" O'Neal asked.

"We kind of got each other," the Gunsmith replied wearily. "But I got him better."

"Obviously," Nagata began. "I was mistaken to assume we were no longer in danger, but—"

The warlord screamed and clamped his left hand to his right wrist. A shaken was lodged in the back of his right hand. One sharp tine had pierced the palm.

Kaiju and O'Neal turned to the ninja who had fallen from the roof. The man in black was propped up on his left elbow as he reached for another throwing star. O'Neal's rifle snarled, and Kaiju launched an arrow. The ninja's body convulsed as both projectiles slammed into his chest.

Kaiju immediately tossed his bow aside and drew his

katana. The samurai didn't hesitate. He swung the sword swiftly. Ultra-sharp steel sliced through Nagata's wrist, cutting off his right hand with a single stroke. The hand fell, the star still jutting from the severed extremity. Nagata shrieked and dropped to his knees, blood gushing from the end of his arm.

"Jesus Christ!" O'Neal exclaimed. "Have you gone bloody mad?"

"Kaiju cut off his hand to save his life," Clint explained. "The ninja dip those stars in poison. The only way to keep it from spreading through Nagata's blood was to amputate—immediately."

Kaiju removed his obi sash and tied a tourniquet to his master's wrist. Mercifully, Nagata passed out. Clint helped Kaiju carry the warlord back to the train.

Rikko attended her father, bandaging his maimed arm with the help of Nagata's remaining concubines. Clint Adams called the rest of the men together for an emergency meeting.

"My name's Josh Washington," the black man explained. "I work here for the railroad. Helps with the trains what need fuel. Those two spooky-men, they come sneakin' into my house 'bout an hour past sunup. Didn't see nothin' until they grabbed me. Tied me up and gagged me. Figured I was a goner for sure."

"Ninja are professional killers," the Gunsmith remarked. "Professionals don't kill innocent bystanders if they can help it."

"Josh said the ninja captured this place in the morning," Kaiju commented. "So Yamato must have sent them last night after he met with you."

"Yeah," Clint agreed. "Yamato must have figured Nagata might refuse to duel with him. So he sent his ninja to arrange a surprise for us. That fella is pretty shrewd.

Must have known we didn't get fuel in Great Dawn and checked a map to figure where we'd go next. Not much escapes Yamato. He probably figured if the ninja didn't stop us, they'd damn sure slow us down.''

''He was right about that,'' Mike O'Neal stated. ''We can't leave until the women finish doctorin' up the boss. You reckon that'll be long enough for the one-eyed bloke to catch up with us, Clint?''

''If he doesn't catch up with us now, he will later,'' the Gunsmith sighed. ''Yamato isn't going to give up.''

''This is true,'' Kaiju agreed. ''Let us confront him here. We'll wait for Yamato to arrive and face him in open combat.''

''I suppose we could set up some sort of ambush,'' O'Neal said. ''That kind of fightin' doesn't appeal to me, but I reckon we don't have a choice.''

''I won't gun down Yamato in cold blood,'' Clint announced. ''That man saved my life back in Great Dawn, and I'll be damned if I'm going to repay him by bushwhacking him.

''No ambush,'' Kaiju agreed with a firm nod. ''It shall be an honorable battle. The victor will claim the *Horseman of Edo* and the loser will claim death.''

THIRTY-TWO

Yamato Fujo and his two samurai henchmen arrived at dusk. Three warriors on horseback, they followed the railroad tracks to the train station. One man carried a bow and arrows, another held a long spear, but Yamato appeared to be armed only with his swords.

"We've been expecting you, Yamato-san," Clint Adams announced in a loud voice as he stepped from the caboose to greet the trio. "About time we settled this business once and for all."

"I do not want to fight you, Mr. Adams," Yamato told him.

"I'm not going to fight you," Clint assured him. "I'm not any good with a sword, and you're no match for me with a gun. The only way we could have a fair fight would be to throw rocks at each other. I don't figure a samurai would consider that an honorable duel."

"Then what do you suggest?" Yamato inquired.

"May I address you, Yamato-sama?" Kaiju Inoshiro asked as he stepped forward and bowed deeply with genuine respect.

"You are Kaiju-san, hai?" the one-eyed samurai inquired. "Nagata-sama's warrior captain. You have a fine reputation as a brave samurai and a man of honor. Please speak, Kaiju-san."

"*Arigato,*" Kaiju nodded. "My master is unable to face you, Yamato-san. He was struck by a ninja shaken, and I was forced to cut off his hand to save his life. He cannot wield a sword, but I am willing to accept the challenge you made yesterday. I will fight in the name of my master."

"Before I decide," Yamato began, "I must know the terms of the duel."

"The terms are all or nothing," Clint explained. "If Kaiju wins, we'll take the *Horseman of Edo* to the president. If you win, the statue is yours to take back to Japan. No tricks. Those are the terms, plain and simple."

"I find the terms acceptable," Yamato declared as he climbed down from his horse. "I shall duel with you, Kaiju-san."

"*Domo arigato,*" Kaiju said, bowing deeply once again. "It is an honor to fight you, Yamato-sama."

To the Gunsmith, it seemed downright bizarre that two men who intended to cut each other to ribbons would be so polite and civil before they drew their swords. Clint figured all pleasantness would cease when the actual duel began.

Kaiju Inoshiro and Yamato Fujo faced each other and exchanged bows. They stood about ten yards apart as they slowly drew their katana fighting swords. Josh Washington had built a campfire to combat the darkness of twilight. The samurai were bathed in yellow light. Their faces were war masks of fury, and shards of fire seemed to dance along the fabulous blades of their honored weapons.

Both men bellowed battle shouts as they charged and attacked. It happened so fast, the Gunsmith wasn't sure which man moved first. It didn't matter because they were both slashing and blocking with uncanny speed and skill.

Steel clanged again and again as neither man could break through the other's defenses.

Suddenly, Kaiju pushed against his opponent's katana, pressing a palm to the unsharpened side of his own blade in order to get a point of leverage. He shoved hard, sending Yamato staggering backward. Kaiju's blade slashed a deft stroke to Yamato's abdomen. Cloth split and a ribbon of blood oozed from Yamato's kimono.

However, the wound was obviously shallow. Yamato's katana blocked Kaiju's next stroke and pressed down on the blade. His sword swiftly cut an upward diagonal stroke which sliced open Kaiju's kimono from rib cage to shoulder. Crimson oozed from Kaiju's chest, but this wound was also shallow, and neither man was ready to slow down.

Swords clashed again and again. Yamato slid his blade forward without warning. The slanted point bit into Kaiju's left biceps muscle. Kaiju retreated with a quick backward gait and Yamato lunged again, eager to keep the upper hand.

Kaiju parried the attack with his katana and pivoted, whirling to the left of his opponent to deliver a sword stroke to Yamato's back. The one-eyed samurai cried out and leaped forward. Blood stained the back of his gray kimono as he jammed the tip of his katana into the ground and appeared to lean on the handle like a crutch.

Kaiju seemed to hesitate. He held his weapon ready, but did not attack. He advanced cautiously. Yamato suddenly whipped his blade upward and flicked dirt into Kaiju's face. Kaiju stumbled backward, blinking his eyes to clear them.

Yamato charged forward and delivered an overhead sword stroke. Kaiju whirled, blocking the other man's katana with his blade. His body weight pushed Yamato's weapon aside. Kaiju's sword suddenly spun in his hands as he reversed his grip on the handle and thrust the blade deep into Yamato's solar plexus. The one-eyed warrior opened his mouth. Blood flowed from his lips.

Kaiju yanked his blade from Yamato's body and pivoted to face his wounded opponent. Yamato dropped to his knees, scarlet spreading across the front of his kimono. He turned his head and gazed up at Kaiju. Yamato weakly nodded as if expressing approval. Then his punctured heart quit beating and he fell, face-first in the dust, and died.

"My God," Mike O'Neal exclaimed. "We won!"

"Yeah," the Gunsmith admitted, unable to feel victory as he gazed down at the body of Yamato Fujo. "But don't ask me to celebrate until we get to Washington and deliver that goddamn statue to the president."

THIRTY-THREE

The following days of their journey to the nation's capital were peaceful, almost dull compared to the excitement and danger before. No one complained. They were all ready for a few days of boredom.

Lord Nagata recovered remarkably well, thanks to the attention of Rikko and the concubine. His daughter made a leather mitten to cover the stump at the end of his right arm. The daimyo seemed to have adjusted quite well to the handicap.

"I'll never have to worry about being challenged to a duel again," Nagata joked. "And the emperor will surely be impressed when he sees how I've sacrificed myself in the line of duty, yes?"

Clint wondered if the emperor would appreciate the fact a lot of other people had sacrificed their lives during the "goodwill mission." Hana, Sakata, Kelly Malone and so many others would be forgotten. But then, who pays much attention to the faceless victims of any war? Had they died in vain? If their spirits could answer, Clint guessed most of them would believe they gave their lives for a good cause.

Perhaps, the Gunsmith mused as the train pulled into a

184

station in Washington D.C. Perhaps the only truth that really matters is what we believe.

"Well, we made it," Rikko remarked as she joined Clint at a window. "A long and dangerous journey, but we made it because of you."

"We made it because of a lot of people," the Gunsmith sighed, still staring out the window although he could see little more than steam from the engine as it grinded to a halt. "Many of them aren't here with us to enjoy this moment."

"If a person is remembered in your mind and your heart," Rikko said softly, "then that person will always be with you. I will always remember you, Clint Adams. In my mind, but most of all in my heart."

"I'm not much for long good-byes," the Gunsmith told her. "You folks are at Washington now. My job is finished. Time for me to collect my wages, get my wagon and horses ready and head back West."

"So soon?" Rikko frowned. "Don't you want to meet the president?"

"I'm sure the president of the United States would be thrilled to know the delegation from Japan was escorted by a fella who's best known as a gunfighter. I'm gonna do your father a favor and spare him that embarrassment. Spare the president, too. Besides, diplomats and politicians speak a different kind of lingo, and I've never been comfortable with it."

"I am tempted to ask if I could go with you," she sighed.

"Please don't," Clint replied, still looking away from her. "That would be a mistake for both of us."

"You are most probably right, Clint," Rikko said sadly. "Then all that remains is for us to say *sayonara*."

"Yeah," he nodded, barely glancing at her face. *"Sayonara*, Rikko."

The Gunsmith walked from the passenger car and didn't look back.